THE ARRIVAL

ERIKA PATTERSON

PART 1

THE MISSION

1

LAST CHANCE

Ella and Martin sat in the exam room quietly. He flipped through a health magazine rapidly, not truly reading any of the article he seemed immersed in. She sat in the hospital shift, slightly chilled, in hopes that the test results would bring them the news they desperately had been waiting for. She looked over at Martin, hoping for momentary eye contact, but he kept them downcast in the magazine. She knew the past few months had been difficult for him, since the fertility treatments and regimen kept him grounded at home.

Ella thought about how she had also made the decision to start a family, which placed her in the position to remain back from the exploratory science missions she had been the primary researcher on for five years. Yet, starting a family was important to her and she knew Martin also wanted children. What she didn't bargain on was that conceiving would be difficult and would take years of trying that had only resulted in multiple disappointments. In this moment she hoped that this would be that moment of success.

When the doctor walked in, she could tell by the look on his face that they were not pregnant. She felt the walls closing in on her as she tried to keep a strong demeanor. Yet, the doctor was telling her information that went beyond her inability to conceive, so she had to remain alert and aware. Couldn't have an emotional breakdown now.

"Your blood tests showed that you will not be able to conceive…ever. Your tests also showed us that you are showing signs of Osteonecrosis. Your x-rays are showing multiple small fractures throughout your limbs, and your bone regeneration has slowed and parts of them have died and are breaking down. With the fragile state of your bones and the advanced rate that this disease is taking, going through pregnancy and birth would probably result in permanent damage. I cannot continue providing you with fertility treatments knowing the damage a pregnancy would cause. I suggest looking for a surrogate or considering adoption," the doctor was direct in his assessment, though it was not the news they wanted to hear. In fact, it was a diagnosis beyond what they expected to receive.

"How advanced is the disease?" She asked.

"Well, without pregnancy or the hormone shots that probably increased the rate of damage, I would suspect it would slow the progression of the disease," he answered.

"Do you think my body could handle going on a mission for the research I have been conducting? Since we are not able to actively conceive a child, and I cannot carry a baby, could we delay finding a surrogate until I go on a mission?" Ella asked, without discussing the situation with Martin. He was staring directly at her without a word of support. He seemed aggravated at her questioning.

"If you want to go on a mission for your research, I suggest you do it within the year. I do not think your body could handle the strain, especially if the disease continues to progress at its current rate."

All Ella heard was that this was her final chance to be able to go on a mission for the research she was invested in. A baby could wait. They could wait and start a family once her mission was complete. Then she could truly take the time to be a mom and invest in the needs of a baby. Martin would just need to understand and wait.

2

MISSION TO BASE CAMP ALPHA

Martin combed Ella's hair back, trying to remember every soft strand cooly sliding through his fingers. She was expected to be gone for the next three months to an off world exploratory camp. This was the woman who he loved deeply and looked forward to having a family with was now taking a different course than what they had planned. He tried to understand, but she had reacted to her diagnosis by throwing herself into her research for the past few months.

Every fiber of her being was focused on getting her body prepared for the strain of traveling through the wormhole. Martin tried discussing their plans for finding a surrogate on her return, but Ella said they needed to wait until her mission was over so she could give all her focus to the research. His patience was thin, but now he just worried about today, the day she would travel to the mission site, not knowing how the pressure of the wormhole travel would impact her body physically.

He pondered how it could damage her and progress her disease further. He wondered if the wife who left today would come back needing assistance that he didn't know if he could manage. Martin was realistic in knowing that Ella may not be physically able to care for a baby once she returned. So, he had been looking at home care nursing services, preparing for the worst.

Ella checked her suit, making sure it was secure and the reinforcements for her body were aligned and not putting pressure in places that would result in an immediate fracture. She gazed up at Martin, noticing the concern he was trying to hide.

"Martin, I'm going to be okay. You'll see me in a few months and we can look at surrogates then. We'll narrow the field down to a few and start contacting a lawyer," she told him with assurance.

"I know. I think I'm just going to miss having you beside me in bed. Maybe now that we aren't trying to have a baby we can be a little adventurous?" He prodded quickly grazing her breast where no one could see.

"Maybe…" she said as she lifted onto her tiptoes and deeply kissed him, ending in a nip of his bottom lip.

This gave Martin hope for the future, and Ella the chance to hold him back from the discussion she wanted to have about possibly not changing their lifestyle by adding a child to the mix. She believed they were both amazing scientists and researchers, and a baby would hinder her, if not both them. After being solely dedicated to her research in the last month, she realized it filled the void that infertility left, a gaping hole that resulted in her feelings of incapability and brokenness.

"I love you," Martin said as Ella situated herself in the two-pilot pod beside her research partner, David. "Take care of her."

"Martin, I will. Nothing will happen to her. I'll make sure to stay with her," David said. "Be there for Ava, will you? She isn't sure how to handle being a researcher's future wife."

Martin assured David that he would watch out for his fiancé as he squeezed Ella's hand and gave a kiss on her helmet before they secured the clear lid of the pod. He watched as the pod slowly made its way to the ready room, and then walked into the waiting area to listen for their transmission that they arrived safely.

Ava was sitting in the waiting room, tears streaming down her cheeks. Her new diamond reflected the lights in the room, creating a forlorn scene of a woman who looked completely abandoned. Martin sat beside Ava, who had dressed to be alluring and sensual for David as he left on the mission. He'd never seen the woman who'd always seemed so naturally simple and plain, dress as provocatively as she was in this moment. He smiled remembering how Ella used to dress up similarly when they went to clubs and she wanted to let him show her off.

Martin reached out and put his arm around Ava, trying to console her. He told her David would be back in three months and things would be fine. But Ava told Martin that they'd had a big fight the previous night. He tried to reassure her that it was only the stress of the mission and that she was welcome to have coffee with him and come over for dinner during the week. He wanted to make sure she didn't feel lonely and that she was welcomed into the astronaut family.

She said she would take him up on that offer. So in the next few months, they got to know each other over weekly coffee meetups and casual dinners out where they would talk about plans for the future with their spouses.

Ella and David arrived safely through the wormhole. Her suit held up well under the pressure and she self checked to make sure there were no significant bruises beginning to emerge on her body. She went to the transmission station and reported back that she and David had made it through safely.

Once there, she and David were assigned quarters where they could put their travel bags, but were needed immediately in the lab to read some of the reports and samples the team had taken earlier in the mission. They determined that some of the samples had strange readings and that more samples needed to be taken, but before they were allowed to go out to take new samples they needed to go through and medical exam and training for expeditions on the surface of the alien world.

Ella headed to the medical ward while David stayed behind continuing to study the vegetation samples that the team had gathered. She was nervous about the impact of the wormhole travel on her body, a fact that she failed to tell David about. All he knew, as her scientific partner and researcher on the project, was that Ella had decided she needed to go on a final mission before she and Martin settled down and started a family.

She approached the medical ward and walked in quietly.

"You must be Ella," the doctor stated. Her name tag had the name Yang on it and her short dark hair, cut in a bob, had bright streaks of red. She looked up and smiled at Ella.

"Yes, I'm Ella Jones," she stated. "I brought my full medical report for you, just in case they failed to get it to you." Ella was concerned that Dr. Yang was not aware or trained to manage her medical condition.

"Yes, I have your reports and x-rays. I suggest you stick

those medical reports and files in your exposition bag in case anything happens out in the field," she suggested.

"Have things happened out in the field before?" Ella asked, wondering if there was a member of her team that needed care that they could only receive back on the base.

"Almost. We almost lost a team in the field because they stayed out too long. I make it a practice now to have all members of the exposition teams carry their medical files with them. There is a colony posting that could help teams out if it is an emergency, and medical files would help them understand a person's medical history — especially yours," she stated directly.

"Yeah, I could see how that would make things easier for them," Ella admitted. She really thought that this was a smart plan that could keep her exposition teams safe when they were out in the field.

"So, what I need from you is an initial x-ray to have a baseline for the travel through the wormhole. I will need to take an CAT-scan once a week to track any progress or changes in your disease. Here's a gown. I need everything off, all metals, clothing. Due to some weird atmosphere on this planet, you will need to take the gown off while in the CAT-scan. Clothing here impedes the readings."

This was unusual, but the issues with instruments on the planet were strange. She remembered that her team stated that their readings in the field were different than the ones they took in the contained lab. So, going through an CAT-scan machine without clothing seemed explainable. She situated herself on the table and attempted to imagine being on a warm beach. Yet, her skin reacted to the cold and she visibly shivered as the CAT-scan began cycling around her.

David arrived for his medical exam as Ella was in the CAT-scan machine. He was taken off guard by her laying in the machine naked. He stood there staring at her, unable to process what was going on, or why she was in the machine without clothing. He realized he had gazed at her for too long and then blushed and looked away.

It wasn't the fact that she was naked, but the last memory he had of her when she was last naked in front of him. That must have been ten years ago, when they were in graduate school in their astrophysics program. He was in love with her and she was dating him to have fun, as she had stated it. He went along with her, in hopes that one day she would realize that she loved him. That day never came, but their nights together, with her dancing uninhibited naked in front of him, until she wrapped herself around him and pushed him into divine ecstasy was the memory that emerged in his mind as he realized he had gazed at her for too long a moment.

"I'll be right with you, Major Gordon," Dr. Yang told him. She seemed unfazed by the fact that he was standing there while a patient, naked, was in her CAT-scan. He thought that this must be normal on such a small camp. He realized that the comfort level between the team may require him to get used to.

The CAT-scan was over and Ella got up and draped the gown back around her. She saw David sitting there and approached him. "What were the sample reading like?"

Of course she asked him about the sample readings. That's Ella, to not react to the fact that he saw her naked in the CAT-scan. To not notice that he was visibly uncomfortable.

"They were unusual. The phosphorus levels were much higher in the field, but the readings in the lab were showing levels that were ten percent lower than the original readings. I really think we need to do our own readings in the field to see what is going on," David explained.

"I agree. Let's get our training completed today and tomorrow so we can get those samples and readings done."

She went behind a curtain and put her clothing back on. Then she left the medical exam room briskly. David sat there deep in thought wondering how he was going to manage working closely with Ella for the next three months, even though he was engaged and she was married. He decided that his only solution was to throw himself into the work.

3

THE STORM

They were cleared to go out into the field after a few days of training. The training took longer than Ella thought, and there were a good many rules to follow if they wanted to make it back to Base Camp Alpha safely. For one, they could only be out on an exposition for six hours at a time. There was a weird anomaly on the planet that distorted time. The six-hour window was the extreme amount of time that teams could go out and come back without disrupting their own time space continuum.

The doctor cleared Ella to go out in the field with Davis, stating that her scans were normal and she did not see any significant changes in her bone density. She grabbed her gear and met David at the rover vehicle. She made sure to put her medical files in her bag to be sure of following the doctor's safety protocols. David had already packed his gear in the rover and had left to get the field equipment for getting the samples. He backed in to the vehicle bay with he equipment in his arms, so she rushed to the door to open it for him.

He smiled at her warmly and thanked her for opening the door. She was grateful to be partnered with her long-time friend on this mission. She felt at ease around him and was able to interact and talk with him naturally. Normally, she felt awkward around other researchers, but David was different. He was the only person she had been able to have a sexual relationship with in graduate school that was based on releasing the stress of school. There were no expectations in their relationship, and when she met Martin, David backed off and respected that she developed romantic feelings for the man who would become her spouse.

Ella thought about Martin, and felt grief and loneliness at leaving him for three months. She knew the nights would end up being the worst for her, since she was used to having him curl up with her. She would miss his warmth.

"Ready to head out? You seem lost in thought," David asked popping her back into the present.

"Yeah, just thinking about home. Let's head out," she answered flatly. David recognized the sadness in her eyes and decided to just let it be. Ella seemed changed in the last six months that they had been working on the research project together. He knew something had changed but Ella was being very quiet about it and he knew if he pushed her to talk, she would argue with him and become cold. That was not a good scenario for communicating with her for the next three months on the research project.

They drove out, with Ella navigating towards the original site where the last expedition team had gathered samples. It was about an hour out to the site, so David activated their timer for six hours to be sure they got back to camp within the allotted time frame.

"So, how is Ava handling you being away for three

months?" Ella asked. David faltered with how direct Ella was able to ask the one question that made him uneasy.

"Not well," he answered looking out at the horizon of the planet.

"Uh oh, paradise ending?" She asked humorously.

"Maybe…We had a fight about me coming on this mission," he stated remembering the jealous reaction that Ava had when she found out that David was going on the mission with Ella.

"Yeah, the first mission is always hard. Martin and I had a hard time with it, especially if our mission times were in conflict. We never saw each other for a long time, beyond a night or two," Ella stated.

"That must have been difficult. I don't think Ava could manage that."

"Well, she isn't a scientist, so she won't have to. All she will have to do is deal with your missions. I know it is still hard to be the one left behind."

"I guess it is," David responded, feeling a bit guilty at judging Ava so harshly and not trying to understand.

"It really is hard. I wasn't able to go on missions, because Martin and I were trying to have a baby. But he thought that meant I was the one grounded, so he kept going on his missions with the geological survey."

"Doesn't it take two people to conceive?" David asked with a sarcastic tone.

"Yeah, but we learned we needed some assistance in that area. I was in fertility treatments and Martin left his contributions with our doctor. Apparently, we weren't timing things right for my body."

"Oh damn, I'm so sorry. But you are on this mission, so what about your treatments?"

"We stopped. They weren't working. I needed a break,

too," she answered without telling him the full reason why she stopped. "So, back to what happened in the fight you had with Ava..."

"Oh, she said that I would get lonely and not be faithful to her. I couldn't promise I wouldn't get lonely, but I did say I wouldn't be unfaithful. I mean we are engaged to be married," he stated emphatically.

"David, I have never seen you act immoral. I don't think Ava needs to worry." He smiled at that statement, wondering how he would reconcile what he told Ava and how he felt at ease with Ella.

One Hour Passed...

They stopped the rover as they got to the site. David got the equipment as Ella set up the temporary shelter, in case there was unexpected weather, which was typical for the planet. After they set up the equipment, Ella started scanning the environment for different sample sites. David sat at the instruments and adjusted the scanners of the surrounding area to get readings of locations they could gather new samples. He also radioed back to Alpha Base Camp to let them know they had reached the destination.

Their suits and breathing apparatus caused them to move a little slower than expected, which frustrated Ella. She wanted to get the new samples and determine the cause of the different phosphorus levels in the readings. She took new samples from the original site and brought them to David. He started measuring their phosphorus and nitrogen levels. While the original samples had similar levels of nitrogen, he still measured that in case there was some impact.

Ella ventured to the first location David marked on the

scan. The ground was a little uneven and she had to walk carefully. She wanted to be sure her decreasing bone density didn't undergo strain that could cause an injury out in the field, especially since David was unaware of her medical diagnosis. She knew it was irresponsible to not inform her research partner, especially since they were going to be taking expeditions into the field together, but she was proud and didn't want to see the pity in his eyes when he looked at her. She already saw that look in Martin's eyes and felt he perceived her as broken and fragile...He even had decreased his sexual interactions with her, and when they were active he was overly gentle. He made her feel broken. She couldn't feel broken with David.

"Okay, I'm at the site. Taking fave samples from Location A," she transmitted to David.

"Are there any water or liquid areas around there to get an additional sample from?" He asked.

"No. I don't see any at this location. Why don't we get soil samples to see if there is something we can identify as a cause," she suggested.

"Sounds good. Your next location will be about fifteen to twenty feet to your right. We are going to go in a circle to each location."

"Okay. Got the samples. Heading to Location B."

As she walked the ground became rockier, though the vegetation remained the same. She needed to walk slower, which impacted the time they had allocated to each location.

Two Hours Passed...

She reached down and started taking the samples. Ella noticed that getting a soil sample was going to be more difficult at this site. She attempted to use the trowel to break up the soil and place it in the sample container.

Meanwhile, David was getting a report that a fast moving storm was headed towards them. It required Ella to come back and for them to get into the temporary shelter.

"Ella, a storm is headed our way. Come back. We need to get under the shelter," David informed her.

"Okay, I need a different tool to get this soil sample anyway. It is not breaking up," she stated. She started heading back, but moved slower due to being careful in the field.

"Ella, you need to move faster than that. The storm is going to be here before you get here at this rate," David said, not understanding why she was moving at this slow pace. This was a woman who could outrun him and was always very efficient with time.

"I'm just trying to be careful. The terrain is rough," she indicated. She did pick up her pace, since she was aware that David took notice of her behavior. He had commented on her moving slower than normal, and she couldn't alert him to anything being different with her. She did notice that her suit was getting fairly warm, so getting in the shelter would allow her to take it off momentarily and cool down.

She got back just as the storm was approaching and they retreated into the shelter. They secured the atmosphere in the shelter and then took their breathing units off to save on air. David noticed that Ella was drenched in sweat and was struggling with getting the suit opened up.

"Let me help you with the fasteners," he suggested. She seemed relieved that he was willing to help her. As he opened up her suit, he noticed that her uniform under the suit was soaked. She was struggling out in the field and he took notice of her physical demand. He peeled the suit off of her and remained quiet as he let her unfasten his suit, though he had no trouble with getting his suit off.

"These are so hard to get off, aren't they?" She stated.

"They really are," he lied, though he agreed with her to hide that he noticed she was struggling. "I'm really hot, too? Aren't you?" he suggested, hoping she would take off the soaked uniform so it could dry out and he could wrap her in an emergency blanket.

"Well, I didn't notice, but I guess I am. My uniform is soaked," she said. What she hadn't noticed was that he poured some of his water down his back to make it appear that he was sweating also.

"Why don't we take our uniforms off to dry out and we can wrap up in the emergency blankets to stay warm," David rationalized. He truly hoped she would tell him what was going on, since they would be out in the field together multiple days while they were at Alpha Base Camp.

"That's a good idea," Ella stated as she unzipped her uniform and peeled it off her body. It left her in her underwear and sports bra, both which were not the standard military issue and provided less coverage than average. He watched her drape her uniform over the boxes as she reached for him to hand over his uniform. He handed it to her, trying to avoid touching her hand. Then he turned around to look for the blankets in their supply box.

"Have you found the blankets?" She asked as she came up behind him and placed her hand gently on his back and leaned over behind him. He body was less than an inch from his, which made him freeze, afraid that if he moved he would make unintended contact with her. He could only find a single blanket. They had only packed one emergency blanket, expecting that there would only be one researcher who would need it in an emergency.

"There is only one blanket," David stated plainly, though he was horrified inside at the predicament he was in. He knew that he could not control how his body physically reacted to her. He never could.

"That isn't a problem. We can share it. We've been friends for a long time."

She reached over him to grab the blanket, not realizing that her breasts grazed his back and her thigh pressed against his side. He shivered from her touch, and she perceived it as him being chilled.

"Come here, you are cold," she said as she wrapped the blanket around his back and stepped into him to use her body heat to warm him up. She pressed herself against him pragmatically, unaware of the effect that she had on him. He groaned softly as his body became aroused.

"I'm sorry," David said immediately. He was embarrassed to have this reaction to her, a married woman and he himself engaged. She smiled at him.

"It's okay, you can't control your body's reaction. We are just trying to stay warm during this storm," she said practically. "Anyway, glad to know I am still attractive to someone."

He looked down at her, trying to read the look in her eyes after saying that. Then he felt a tear fall on his chest. He wrapped his arms around her and hugged her to him, hoping he could help her feel better. She wrapped her arms around his back and buried her face into his chest. He'd forgotten how small and petite she felt in his arms, though he knew how strong she was. Her tight waist tapered in slightly from her hips and then accentuated the voluptuous breasts and plump rear that gave her the appearance of an hourglass.

He felt her tears falling on his skin silently. He reached for her chin and lifted her face up towards him. She looked up at him and the heartbreak revealed in her eyes swallowed his heart whole. He wiped away her tears with his thumb and kissed her forehead gently. The storm raged outside their shelter, making communication with Alpha Base Camp impossible.

"Let's sit together," she suggested. He sat down and expected her to sit down beside him. Instead, she sat in from of him, facing him, wrapping her legs and arms around his body. She nestled her face into his neck. Her body was almost completely pressed against his in the familiar embrace from years ago.

Three Hours Passed...

He struggled with her closeness, trying to just hold her and help her feel better, cared for. He leaned down and pressed his lips against her shoulder, not knowing if he was reading her body language correctly. She nipped his neck gently with her teeth and squeezed her body closer to his, pressing her pelvis into his.

She moaned in the midst of her crying, sounding like a sob caught off with some other emotion. He grabbed her hips and pressed her in, letting her know how desirable she was to him. She reacted to him physically by rubbing her body against him. He pulled her bra over her head and she reached down to pull his member free of his underwear.

In a swift moment, she held her panties to the side and plunged him deeply inside of her. He was taken off guard by her actions, abandoning all thoughts of faithfulness to Ava. All that mattered was this moment, the need to make Ella feel desired, the desire to bury himself inside of her as long as he could. She was forceful and intense as she rode him as hard as she could. The storm raged on.

He turned her over, pulled her panties and his underwear off completely, and buried himself behind her as she arched up to him on her hands and knees. He pounded her, making up for years lost imagining himself with her. She screamed out shivering and he felt her spasm and tighten. He kept thrusting and soon spilled himself into her.

They lay there spent, unable to look each other in the eyes. They wondered what they had just done and how they would explain themselves to the people they loved back home, the two people they were devoted to. Yet, Ella hadn't felt a release like this in over a year. She had felt abandoned in her desire, a sense that there was no expectation to be something more. He had wanted her, just her. David felt like he was able to provide her with the things she needed in this moment. He knew she had no expectations for the future, she never had.

They lay there in silence, not touching each other.

Four Hours Passed...

The storm eased and their uniforms were dry. They got dressed with their backs turned to each other. They suited back up and went outside the shelter. They decided they needed to pack up the equipment and supplies and return the next day for the rest of the samples.

The ride back to Base Camp Alpha was quiet. They were deep in their own thoughts looking out the windows as David drove back. As they approached the camp David cleared his throat to get her attention.

"So, what happened out there..." he started.

"It happened. We got each other through the storm. Yes?" She suggested.

"I guess we could call it that…" he responded.

"We are calling it that," she said. "It was a horrible storm, worst than we expected."

David didn't know if Ella was talking about the actual storm or something more.

4

MARTIN & AVA

Martin planned to meet Ava for their weekly dinner meeting. It had been a few weeks since Ella and David had left. He was looking forward to the end of the three months for Ella to be home, but at the same time he was nervous about her response that he had already started looking at surrogate women to carry their child. In fact, if she had left her eggs he could have chosen a surrogate and surprised her with an upcoming pregnancy.

Before the dinner he had a scheduled video chat with Ella, which he looked forward to. He logged on to the system and waited to make contact with the station. The familiar static interference in the transmission began and he saw the control center commander make contact.

"Good afternoon, Mr. Jones," the commander greeted.

"Hi! How's things going there?" Martin asked.

"They are fine, a little stormy, but we are making progress on the samples," he answered.

"How's Ella doing? Anything unusual happening?"

Martin asked, trying to see if her commander noticed any uncharacteristic behavior from her.

"She's doing great. Her work is phenomenal. She's really dedicated," he answered.

"Oh that is good. I'm so proud of the work she is doing. Her and David," Martin stated.

"So, that's what I wanted to talk to you about. She and David had to make an unexpected expedition trip after a big storm the other day. It delayed them getting the samples they needed," the commander informed Martin.

"So, she isn't there?" Martin asked.

"No, she isn't. She left a message to let you know she was really sorry," he relayed.

"So, can we get in contact later today?" Martin asked.

"Unfortunately, no. We will be out of transmission abilities. The planet is orbiting behind its sun. We are expected to be out of transmission capabilities for the rest of their mission. We may even need to coordinate and be flexible with timing on their return," he informed.

"So, I won't be able to talk with her for the whole mission? No contact? Was she aware of this?" He asked.

"Yes. She was aware and was very sorry that she couldn't be here for this transmission," he answered.

"I see. I can't say I'm not disappointed, but you can't help the rotation and orbit of a planet," Martin stated with some uplifting attitude that he didn't truly feel. The transmission ended and Martin threw his glass of sherry across the room.

His plan to talk with her about surrogates backfired — she wasn't even available to talk and communicate with him for three months. He didn't understand why she would decide that a field expedition she had two months to complete was more important than talking with her husband the only chance they had to communicate for her whole mission.

He met Ava at the restaurant. As expected, she was a mix of distraught and angry. She combatted her emotions by presenting herself in a very attractive way. Martin noticed her appearance and approached her slowly.

Her long chestnut hair fell is soft waves down her bare back. The dress plunged down beyond the small of her back. The loose fabric swayed open in increments to the side, revealing the curves of her hips. The dress was cut so low, that he couldn't see any sign of her wearing undergarments of any sort without being revealed.

When she turned towards him and smiled, the royal blue dress draped low between her cleavage down beyond her breasts and had slits up her legs that stopped just below where her hips and legs met. Her stiletto heels caused the calves in her legs to curve in a shapely way. Martin wondered how David met such a beautiful woman, a ballet dancer, with the schedule he kept as a scientist. Martin didn't even know David had an interest in dance.

Ava swayed towards him like a cat stalking her prey. Martin was aware of the creature approaching him. He attempted to reach out cordially to her, to be a gentleman and polite, so she wouldn't take his interactions in an inappropriate way. Yet, she embraced him on her approach and kissed him seductively. Then she whispered in his ear.

"So, let's pretend that I am Mrs. Jones tonight. Let's act as if we were married. They won't know we aren't. What do you say?" She suggested with her left leg softly rubbing against his thigh and her fingers entwining in his.

"I can play this game tonight. But are you sure you really want to play?" He asked.

"Absolutely," she stated leaning her body into his. He placed his hands on the small of her back, caressing the bare skin slowly, while leaning down and kissing her deeply. She moaned and pulled away with a sly smile. Martin was pleasantly surprised and distracted by the playful game she suggested, which was a nice diversion to the disappointment that Ella presented him with. He suspected that Ava's game was a reaction to the lack of communication with David.

They approached the hostess. "I have the private room reserved for Mr. Jones and myself. It is our anniversary," Ava told her. She looked back to Martin and smiled slowly.

"Right this way, Mr. and Mrs. Jones," the girl replied leading them to the back of the restaurant to a room that was private from the rest of the clientele. They sat in the curved booth a small distance from each other. Then the hostess explained the process for ordering from the private room.

"You will press these buttons on the wall to let your server know what you desire to order. Your bottle of wine will be delivered through this delivery site. They will press a button and spin the wine and glasses to you. Your meal will be delivered through this slot. This room is completely private and soundproof. We have white noise machines built into the walls so no one can hear your conversations and interactions. You will completely private and concealed." She smiled and left the room handing Ava the golden key on a chain. Ava closed the door, inserted the key, and turned it until Martin heard a click.

Ava turned around and faced Martin with a seductive smile, trailing her fingertips down her cleavage. Martin followed her fingers with his eyes and trailed them down her body. He felt a pang of guilt and looked away. Then the wine swiveled in with the tinkle of two glasses vibrating against each other.

"I took the liberty of preordering for us. The less interruption and decision making, the better. I would hate for us to get too distracted in our game tonight," she told him as she poured the wine in the glasses for them. He looked at her, wondering why his wife couldn't be this commanding and sensual. Ava made Ella seem cold and distant.

"What did you order?" He asked.

"Does it matter?" She answered as she slid into the booth next to him. He shook his head *no*. "So, what would you do to your wife in a private room like this?"

"I would kiss her," he answered. She leaned into him and began kissing him. He seemed stiff and unsure of what to do next.

"What else?" She asked in a deep whisper.

"I may hug her and put my arm around her," he answered.

"I think we can be more creative than that," Ava stated. Martin was taken off guard, wondering how he would manage himself in this situation. They were playing a game, but Ava seemed to be playing a game that Martin was unprepared for.

"I'm not sure we should-" She kissed him as he spoke and gently scraped her nails in his hair.

"Mr. Jones, don't think, just act. Do what you have always wanted to do to Mrs. Jones." Which inspired Martin to think about all the things Ella had never allowed him to try.

He pulled Mrs. Jones to his lap to straddle him. He kissed her neck as she moaned and then took liberties to bite her with force that he knew would leave a mark. She scrapped her nails down his back, indicating he was arousing her. Her nipples were tight and she arched back to show him her body's reaction to him. He reached up and cupped her breasts, grazing his thumbs back and forth over her nipples, making them tighter and harder.

Then she reached down and grazed her hand along his groin before beginning to fumble with the closure of his pants. It took only a moment for her to release his arousal and set him free. Then he felt her connect her sex to his, rubbing her slick folds along his shaft. She was deliberate, rubbing herself along him, teasing the tip of his shaft with the hint of her warmth, but never allowing him entrance.

"I need you," he said in torture. She smiled.

"What is it you need?" She asked, continuing to rub herself along him. Then she let her dress fall down over her shoulders, revealing her high, tight breasts. She pushed him down to the booth in complete control of the situation.

"I need to feel you," he answered.

"In what way do you need to feel me?" She asked.

"Around me. I want to be inside of you."

"Oh, that. Are you sure?"

"In this moment, yes." He needed to feel sex again. He knew she needed it too, he could feel her arousal.

"Then I'm yours, my husband," she said still playing the game, playing her role, and plunging herself around him, enveloping his shaft to the core of her being. She rode him hard, spasming around him until he poured himself into her.

Then she lay back, spent in the moment. Martin felt satisfied more than he had felt in the past year. He suspected it was due to the risk and excitement they had just taken. Then he realized he wanted this game to continue, but was unsure of how to proceed.

Ava repositioned her dress, pulled out underwear from

her purse, and pulled them on. That was the signal to Martin that he, too, should readjust his clothing and act as if nothing happened. He sat wondering where the food Ava had ordered was as she lounged drinking a glass of wine.

"So what did you order for us?" He asked spiritedly.

"Me." She reached for the key, turned it. "See you next week. Text me where we should eat." Then she walked away leaving Martin stunned.

He felt uneasy about what had happened between them. Martin made sure he arranged all their dinner meetups ahead of time in very public locations that were casual and gave them no opportunities for intimacy. It was difficult for him, since he was attracted to Ava and she made sure she was alluring, but Martin held fast to remaining chaste until Ella returned home.

5

TRAVEL HOME

Ella and David were scheduled for a trip back home She had to take a final CAT-scan to get a baseline reading on the progression of her disease. The doctor seemed satisfied with her findings and released Ella to travel back through the wormhole and back.

She gathered her bags to travel home and looked forward to getting home and seeing her husband, hoping that reconnecting with him would help her feel more in tune with him as a wife. She was feeling guilt at the weak moment she had in the field with David. They had not addressed what happened, feeling truly uncomfortable with the situation.

She arrived at the pod that they would travel in to go through the wormhole. David glanced up at her and smiled warmly. She glanced down at the floor acting like there was nothing happening. As she lifted her bag swiftly she felt a pull that strained her arm. He noticed and grabbed her bag before anyone else would notice. She looked up at him and he gazed directly into her eyes, letting her know that he saw her. Saw her struggle and her truth.

A single tear fell. Her lashes glistened with emotion. She sighed deeply in secret distress, knowing her travel back through the wormhole and back may be her last mission. He put his hand on her back and gently helped her into the suit that was reinforced. He didn't mention that he noticed the suit was made differently than his, though the reinforcements were covertly hidden in the seams of the suit.

She climbed in the pod and he settled in beside her. The lid was closed and they were guided toward the wormhole. He switched his transmission to just between the two of them.

"Ella, what is going on?" He asked.

"Nothing," she answered.

"I will not argue with you, but you are struggling physically," he stated directly.

"It's between my doctor and me," she said.

"Ella, I have been going out on expeditions with you. You have been going slower than normal. You are being more careful than usual, which I don't mind. But things are taking longer than the calculated for," he presented sternly.

"I'm just being careful," she said.

"Okay, then let's talk about the elephant in the room. We had sex in the field," he said.

"It was a weak moment," she said.

"Ella, you are never weak. What happened that caused you to even have a weak moment?" He asked.

"It doesn't matter anymore," she said.

"I suspect it has something to do with Martin. You decided to insist on taking an expedition when we were supposed to have a transmission with Martin and Ava. I felt really bad about it, but you seemed unaffected by the decision."

"Yeah, and?"

"I have known you for over ten years. You don't react that way unless there is an ulterior motivation. So, spill it." He demanded.

"I can't have children, and Martin wants children. I would risk becoming disabled if I even carry a child. My bones will shatter in the birth, if I can manage carrying a baby to term. But that doesn't matter, I can't even get pregnant."

He was taken off guard. He hadn't realized how distressing the situation was or how much she had undergone while they had worked side-by-side the past nine months.

"Ella, I am so sorry. How can I help you on this return home?" He asked her, concerned about how she would react to Martin.

"Can you go to the doctor with me if Martin can't go?" She asked.

"Absolutely! What type of appointment will it be?" He asked thinking of how it would be awkward if it were her fertility treatment doctors.

"The doctor doing the CAT-scans to keep track of the progress of my disease," she answered.

"What is this disease exactly?" He asked.

"Osteonecrosis,' she said.

"Oh, so necrotic? What exactly is dying with your bones and what does that do?"

"Apparently, blood flow is being blocked by minute fractures that can only be detected via CAT-scan at this point. But when the blood flow is blocked that section of bone starts to die and become weaker."

"Is that why you kept getting CAT-scans every week?"

"You knew?"

"It was unusual. No one else got them."

They arrived at the end of the wormhole. When Ella started to get out of the pod, she felt her hips and upper legs ache unusually. David helped her out, taking on the weight she placed on him without letting anyone else know. He grabbed their gear and placed it on the rolling cart. She was limping slightly as they approached the waiting area that Martin and Ava were sitting in.

Martin saw her walk through the door and began walking towards her. He noticed her limp and looked at David, who gave him a knowing look. Martin realized then that David knew about Ella's diagnosis. Ella smiled at Martin hopefully and leaned into him for a kiss. David glanced away feeling confused at seeing her kiss her husband.

Ava walked over, "Miss me?" She asked.

"Yes. Yes I did," David said with a warm smile towards her. Maybe all that happened on the planet was insignificant and not actually an issue that carried weight. He decided that this was the life he left behind and was returning to. This was the life that mattered in the long run. He embraced her and kissed her. She responded in kind, but seemed a little distant.

Ava looked over David's shoulder and made eye contact across the room with Martin. He looked back at her and smiled, then help his finger to his lips to indicate she should remain quiet about their evenings. She smiled in acknowledgement and gave him the "okay" sign with her hand.

6

WELCOME HOME

Martin took Ella home to their house overlooking the coast. She went out to the deck and inhaled the crisp sea air. He came up behind her and leaned in while kissing her neck. She leaned back against him and smiled.

"I missed you," he whispered.

"It did feel like a long time. Weird, since we've been apart that long in the past," she commented. He noted mentally that she had not stated that she missed him.

"So, what would you like to order? I was thinking the local steakhouse was a good choice. Something to celebrate you being home," he suggested.

"Mmm, that and a nice blush wine. We didn't have wine on the planet. Amazing the things you miss," she said taking a deep breath in and holding her arms out to feel the cool breeze off the coast.

"I take it you missed the sea," he stated with a chuckle.

"Oh, so much. It smells different on that planet. Somewhere between ozone and sulphur with a hint of dirt. I can't imagine anything that smells like that," she said.

Martin pulled her hair off her neck gently, and the planetary essence drifted up to him. He laughed.

"Okay, yeah, your hair has an interesting smell. How about we open up the windows in our bathroom, get in the shower, and let me scrub off the essence of that planet from your body and out of your hair?" He suggested.

"As long as we can order dinner afterwards. I want some juicy steak!" She said. He nodded as he took her hand and led her slowly to the bathroom.

He opened the windows and turned around to her. She was moving slowly, almost struggling, as she was removing her clothing. He came over to her and shook his head at her letting her know it was his job to remove her clothing.

He slowly pulled off her top and unbuttoned her pants as he leaned in for a slow, sensual kiss. He could feel her smile under his kiss and she responded with an urgent need, leaning into his body. Her pants slipped to the floor around her ankles and she stepped out of them. She was now standing in her bra and underwear that were always a little skimpier than the military requirements.

Her skin was paler than when she left on her mission, and had a blueish undertone. He noticed a few faint bruises around her pelvis that concerned him, considering her disease and how it could be progressing. He refrained from saying that he noticed her bruises, not wanting to make her feel broken while they were intimate. So, instead, he unclothed himself and presented himself to her in his full glory.

She reached out to caress him and hugged herself to him. She began wrapping her leg around him and pulling herself up to have her torso line up with his for optimal coupling, but he pulled her off and guided her into the shower. He walked into the shower with her and reached for the shampoo.

He unbraided her hair and began washing her long hair gently, massaging her scalp. Then he rinsed the shampoo out, wiping the suds from her hair off her body, gliding his hands down her breasts and hips. He then grabbed the soap and washed her body from neck to feet with his hands, paying special attention to the folds between her legs and the curve of her rump.

Once he rinsed the soap off her body, he knelt at her feet and urged her to sit on the stone bench in their shower. He kissed her mound and flicked the pearl hidden in her folds with his tongue. She moaned, reaching out to the walls of the shower. He buried his tongue inside of her and nipped at her pearl, waiting on her response, which caused her to tense up in expectation. Then he moved his tongue in a rhythm with her response, building her desire until she shuddered under his ministrations.

He quickly lifted her and pressed her against the wall and she wrapped her legs around his waist. He penetrated her in an intense plunge, pulling her hips down on top of him. He pounded into her over and over until he spilled himself into her, reminding her body of how it belonged to him and needed him completely.

In that moment of her husband thrusting into her, with the sound of the water falling, she remembered the storm and the shelter and David filling her up completely. Making her feel like she was stretched and remolded to fit his sex. Hitting sensual nerves she hadn't felt in the years of marriage, the years she felt she had been satisfied. Though she orgasmed this evening, the intensity waned in the familiarity of marital bonding and comfort with knowing she was cared for, though not brought to the intense desire she'd always felt with David.

7

EVERYDAY SCHEDULES

Ella woke the next morning after a warm and relaxing night with Martin. She went into the kitchen and began making the coffee he typically had each morning and began working on the breakfast she only made on special occasions. She was happy to be home as she mixed the batter and heated the griddle on the stove.

Martin walked in with a binder that he placed on the table. He grabbed a coffee mug and kissed Ella's cheek. She flipped the pancakes and served them to him as they were ready. Once a few more were cooked, she sat down with him to eat.

"What's the binder for?" She asked taking a sip of her coffee.

"Well, I took it upon me to begin narrowing down the choices of surrogates for us. I thought that would make the process a little easier for us," he stated.

"Oh, that was a good idea. Efficient. So, should I flag the ones I like?" She asked.

"Yes, that would work. Then we can look at the ones

you chose and narrow them down to three," he explained. "I can look at your choices once I get home from the lab this evening."

Ella knew he had responsibilities at his own lab and with his own research, but she was still a little disappointed that he was not staying at home her first day back home. She got up and walked him to the door and kissed him bye. The schedule was as if she had never been off on a mission. It was normal, expected, easier to fall back into when things were as scheduled.

After he left for the lab, Ella poured another cup of coffee, grabbed the binder, and walked out on the deck. She wanted to be in the sunlight, her favorite location of their home. She sat in the lounge chair and perused the binder of surrogates. All the surrogates fit a certain stereotype. They all had dark hair, pouty lips and blue eyes, and were very buxom. This made Ella smirk, wondering what Martin had actually been looking for in a surrogate.

So, Ella began looking at their medical histories to determine if there were some of the women she could weed out. She first wanted to eliminate women who had never been surrogates before or had given birth. She discovered a few who seemed to be good candidates, and each of those women were absolutely beautiful. She wondered why Martin had chosen so many beautiful women as surrogate options, unless he didn't think she would produce viable eggs.

Then she read their files closer. Apparently they were listed as surrogates willing to undergo natural conception with a couple. Natural conception. That phrase stuck out to Ella. It sickened Ella to even think about the way Martin wanted to conceive a child. He expected her to be intimate with him and another woman while he conceived a child with the surrogate during sex. Ella tossed the binder on the table, as she began crying over how this process made her feel broken and incapable.

8

THE CAT SCAN

Ella called David to let him know she was ready to go for her medical check. She told him that she didn't want to inconvenience Martin by asking him to take a day off from his lab to go with her to get a CAT scan and update on her condition. What she actually wanted was to go with someone who didn't view her as broken.

David picked her up at her house. He took her to the base hospital for her scheduled CAT scan and check up. She was naturally beautiful as she walked out of her house and to his car. Her hair was in her customary braid that swayed as she walked. The highlights shown in her hair as the sun shone down on her, lighting her up with its warmth. David had forgotten how beautiful she shown in the sunlight.

She greeted him with a smile and kissed his cheek. Her blouse gaped open slightly as she leaned in to kiss his cheek, and David couldn't help but notice the sheer lace bra revealed to him. He knew she had no concept the impact she had on him. She walked around and got in his car and he started the engine up.He'd driven his muscle car, taking advantage of the month they had home before heading back off world.

He waited with her after the CAT scan. Then her doctor came out and called her back. This doctor was new and asked if her husband would like to join them as he motioned to David. She told him that she would like it if her husband joined her in the room. David looked at her startled, but her stern look back to him let him know that he was to play along and pretend he was her husband.

The doctor informed her that her disease was progressing. She would be cleared for a final mission only at the rate of progression and the toll it was taking on her body. David held her hand as she received he news. The doctor put his hands on top of theirs and stated how sorry he was to be giving her — them — this news.

David pulled her in to his arms as the doctor walked from the room and kissed the top of her head. They heard the doctor quietly tell the nurse to give them a moment alone in the room. She collapsed in his arms and cried. He just held her, waiting on her to calm down or settle before they walked out to his car to leave. But he didn't realize that she was holding him, savoring the time she had to hold him and be held by him — precious time she knew she would never have once she and Martin had a baby. Time forever lost once David married Ava.

9

SCIENCE MISSION

Ella gave Martin the news about her prognosis. She let him know that she believed they should wait until after her third and final mission before making a decision about a surrogate. He asked if she would at least be willing to have her eggs harvested and frozen for the future. She asked him to give her time to think about it.

He told her that they didn't have the time for her to think about it, since she was only home for a month from her mission. In fact, he had scheduled an appointment with their fertility doctor and had the hormone shots ready to give her for egg harvesting. She felt cornered by him, since he had scheduled and gone through all this planning and effort.

So, Ella agreed to go the next day with Martin to her doctor for the procedure to harvest a few of her eggs. Martin gave her the shot and kissed her passionately. They headed to bed and he paid special attention to her, making sure she was sexually satisfied, though they were prohibited from having intercourse.

Afterward, she curled up on her side with him scooped

around her back and quietly let her tears fall onto her pillow, knowing that tomorrow would give him access to choose one of the surrogates from the binder while she was off world.

THE NEXT MORNING found them at the hospital preparing for Ella to go under anesthesia for the egg harvesting procedure. It would only be a twilight sleep, but with her prognosis they preferred to do the procedure in the hospital for any safe guards they needed to possibly have access to. Martin squeezed her hand and smiled at her, telling her she was going to be great. He truly looked excited about her having the procedure.

What she wasn't informed of was that he was off to a room to ejaculate into a cup so the doctor could fertilize her eggs within the week. Martin had already made a plan to hire one of the surrogates from the binder and have her move in to the guest room. He would make sure she was cared for and lived in a safe place, since she would be carrying his child.

Ella wished she could be as excited as he was as she counted backwards and the light above her dimmed.

SHE AND MARTIN left the hospital after she was fully awake from her procedure. She seemed fairly numb, though had slight twinges of cramping from the needle punctures. She'd never realized how much harvesting her eggs would hurt afterwards. She was also nauseous from the anesthesia. She'd never handled anesthesia well.

"Now we will be ready for your return to have a baby.

Did you pick out some of the surrogates I can draft a contract with, yet?" Martin asked, knowing she'd thrown the binder off to the side of their deck.

"Not yet," she answered blandly.

"Don't worry. I can do that if you need me to. I know how this could be too emotional, especially with the hormone injections," he stated, knowing exactly which surrogate he actually wanted.

He'd already chosen her and had a preliminary introduction to him. In fact, he'd already met face-to-face with a few of the surrogates the company provided for men who wanted to interact with the surrogate to attempt a natural conception scenario. Ella was disgusted by the idea after reading the profiles and the process of what the company called "natural conception." She wanted no part of that interaction, though Martin seemed insistent that this was the best choice for them.

"Sure, just handle it all. I'm not actually here to make all the appointments. So, you should make the appointments so we can go to them in three months after I am back," she conceded. Martin was thrilled she just gave him the option of handling all the details.

Once home, Ella laid down to sleep off the rest of the anesthesia effects.

~

Ella awoke to Martin on the phone. He sounded tense. He seemed to be trying to keep his voice down. She dozed back off to sleep.

The next morning she awoke to find Martin packing up his bag.

"What's going on?" She asked, finding a cup of coffee waiting for her on the night stand.

"I got called off on a mission. I tried to get out of it, but they insisted that I go since I was the lead researcher," he answered. "I'm really sorry about this."

"Can it wait a couple weeks until I head back?" She asked.

"No, it can't. Just like you just had to go out and get those samples instead of making the transmission call home.. It is the same thing," he answered.

"Actually, no it isn't. We were running behind on our sample collections and were under a time crunch. Your missions are geological and aren't going anywhere," she said.

"Well, I just don't see it that way. I have to go. Just deal with it," he said as he jammed clothes into his bag.

"We can't have a baby together if neither of us is available to parent. We also can't decide on a surrogate if we fail to spend the time we have together actually together," she debated.

"I have to go," he said.

"Will you be back before I leave on my mission?" She asked.

"No, they told me it would be at least a month that I would be in the field," he said directly. He leaned in for a kiss and a hug. She allowed him to kiss her, but remained distant in her reciprocation. She was angry at him, especially after pressuring her to undergo an egg harvesting procedure and choosing how their surrogate would be. He walked out the door and she slumped on the couch and cried.

10

COMFORT AND SUPPORT

"David, Martin just left on a mission for a month. He left after we argued. Are you free to get a beer?" Ella asked him over the phone.

"Yeah, I am. Ava and I aren't doing so great right now," he answered.

"See you at Harvey's in fifteen?" She asked.

"Bet I can beat you there!" He joked.

Ella threw on her jacket and shoved her feet into her shoes rushing to the door. Then she stopped and thought about how she looked. A ponytail and sweatpants showed she was desperate and in distress. The mascara smeared under her eyes showed she'd been crying. She didn't want David to see her as a pitiful, frumpy woman pining over her husband.

So, she hopped in the shower to scrub down her body and get the makeup off her face. She braided her red hair in a long braid down her back. Then she chose a short skirt, lacy thin lingerie, and a slightly sheer top that would give hints of the lace underneath. She put on her heels, mascara, and red lipstick, knowing her natural beauty, bare legs, and pouty lips would be alluring and sexy. She needed to be seen as sexual instead of pitiful.

As she reached for her wedding band, she hesitated, then left it in the dish it occupied. Instead, she put on a ring her mother had given her that she'd worn all through college and grad school.

She left for the bar…

Ella strolled into Harvey's, her heels clicking slightly on the wood floor. David looked towards her and smiled. He wore tight jeans that accentuated his butt and a loose sweater that would reveal his collarbone as he shifted towards her. She approached him as he got off his stool at the bar. He greeted her with a hug and kissed her cheek.

She sat on the stool beside him, which hiked her skirt up, revealing almost all her thighs to him. She swiveled her stool towards him, and he struggled to keep his eyes lifted towards her face, knowing she left herself open to his gaze with her legs slightly parted in the way she sat on the stool and leaned towards him. Her knees clashed with his, so she moved her position to have one of his knees between hers, which caused her to sit with her legs open to him, the skirt hem keeping her in shadow though enticing.

"Let me buy you a drink," she offered.

"Okay, whiskey on the rocks," he ordered.

"I'll have what he's having," she said with a sly smile to him. He noticed she wasn't wearing her wedding band and his heart leaped uncontrollably. He grabbed her hand and caressed her fingers, especially grazing the one that held her wedding band. The bartender served them their drinks. Ella slammed her down and ordered another.

"Hey, slow down," David said.

"Not tonight. Please, I need to drink," she said.

They sat and drank, telling each other about the fights they had with their partners. David revealed that he and

Ava were calling off the engagement, since things were not working out with him being away on missions. Ella placed her hands on David's legs and leaned in to him to express how sorry she was about that situation. Instead of her expressing her sorrow, she kissed him, tasting him, languishing in his response to her.

He spotted a table in the corner dimly lit and suggested they go sit over there. It was fairly private and he could block her being seen in that corner. The bartender brought them more drinks and placed a key under David's glass. The hostess recognized what the bartender had done and approached David and Ella.

"Excuse me, we have a private booth that could be of better service for you." She guided them to a room in the back, gave David directions for ordering, and placed the key in his hand. He didn't know what to make of the room with a booth and door that locked, but he locked the door to insure their privacy, Then Ella sat down in front of him and pulled him to her, laying back in front of him.

He reached out and grabbed her waist, pulling her to him, and pressing his leg into her mound. He could feel her heat through his jeans. He unbuttoned her slippery blouse revealing her lace bra that barely contained her plump breasts. He leaned towards them and pulled the edge of the bra down with his teeth to release her nipple. He sucked on it hard, causing her to moan in response. He was rock hard in that moment.

He tore open his jeans and pushed everything he had on down, slid her lace thong to the side, and thrust himself inside of her. She wrapped her legs around his waist and held on to him as he thrust into her, making her spasm around him. Every time she spasmed he thrust harder to meet her and cause her to react with more intensity. Then he couldn't hold back his own pleasure and released his desire into her.

David rode with Ella in her Uber to be sure she made it home safely. He didn't go inside with her and she didn't invite him in. He then rode home and headed to bed.

Ella woke the next morning with an intense headache. She was also hurting a bit more from procedure. She felt intense pings with cramping and determined she needed to reset from the procedure and drinking the previous night.

11

RETURNING TO THE MISSION

Ella and David headed back to the mission a week after Martin left on his mission. In the pod, David caressed her hand with his, eventually intertwining his fingers with hers. She gazed at him longingly through the helmet and then looked away as a tear slid down her face.

When they arrived she checked in with the doctor. Ella let the doctor know about the procedure for harvesting her eggs and that she just felt tired from it. The doctor told her that she could waive the CAT scan today and just have Ella go to her quarters and rest. Ella did exactly that and fell asleep from emotional exhaustion.

Ella and David headed out for their first mission back the day after they returned to Alpha Base Camp. She was still feeling sore from the egg harvesting procedure and wondered why she was reacting so badly from it. As usual, they silenced the headsets from transmitting their conversation back to the camp.

"You okay, Ella?" David asked, noticing she seemed to be physically agitated.

"Yeah, just sore," she answered.

"Did you work out too much while we were back home? Maybe have a stress fracture?" He asked with concern.

"No, I had that egg harvesting procedure Martin wanted."

"Whoa, you didn't tell me that the other night. Why'd you do that? I thought you two planned to wait."

"I did, too. But I was wrong in how he felt. I let him pressure me into it. I'm mad that I did it. I've been really sore since the procedure."

"Did they do something wrong in the procedure?"

"I don't know. I know the hormone shot Martin gave me was the night before the procedure. Something about forcing my eggs to develop early for the harvesting. I was fine after the shot and they said they got a few."

"I wonder how long the hormone is active." David pondered.

"They said a few days. I'm probably sore from the hormone forcing me to ovulate."

"I bet that is the reason. So if you are able to ovulate, what was the fertility issue?"

"Martin didn't have good swimmers and needed help. Then we found out about the bone disease and determined I wouldn't be able to carry a child to term safely."

David felt nauseous, thinking about the night in the bar. Thinking about how they didn't plan on having sex. Thinking about her body wrapped around his. Thinking it was safe since she was unable to get pregnant. Knowing all his assumptions were wrong, yet remembering how amazing they felt buried in each other.

"Maybe I can figure out a treatment to help you not be

so sore. My med kit is stocked pretty well," David suggested.

She smiled at him, knowing he meant well. The reached their location in record time.

About three hours into the mission, Ella ran across what looked like algae in a crevice of a rock formation. She called David over, since it was in a dark location and she was unsure of how far in the rocks she should go. He followed her in with a light source to help them navigate.

He took an atmosphere reading in the formation and determined that they could save their oxygen tanks and breathe the air. So they took their helmets off and in order to work easier with collecting the samples in the dark, took their protective suits off.

As always, Ella was sweating more than normal and expected. She attempted to cool down by unbuttoning the top portion of her uniform, taking it off, and letting it fall from her waist. This left her with just her sports bra on, since she never wore the standard issue t-shirt under her uniform. They worked closely together in silence. Then his external light started flickering and went out.

The lack of light required them to remain in constant contact with each other in order to complete taking the samples. Her contact with him was arousing, but he remained focused on the task at hand. His contact with her made her abdomen twinge and release a heat between her legs, making her shift awkwardly and flush visibly. She was grateful they were in complete darkness.

Once completing the samples, she pulled her uniform back up and they both put their protective suits and helmets back on. They rode back to Alpha Base Camp in silence, not knowing what to say to each other.

AFTER DINNER, Ella and David decided to take a walk around the base together. There was a lookout post that provided a large window that overlooked the valley below. It was absolutely beautiful. They could see in the far distance at night the dim light on the horizon where the permanent colony resided. The lookout post was typically empty and provided them with the privacy to talk, without the cramped quarters of their rooms. Ella like wide open areas, like her deck overlooking the ocean back home. The lookout post gave her a sense of that openness.

The window not only overlooked the valley, but also curved up to see the sky above. They could quietly lay there and watch the stars in this planet's galaxy, wondering how many constellations the colony would develop in order to track the movement of the stars here. David went to grab the stash of pillows and blankets in the closet and lay them out for them to stargaze.

Ella locked the door to the overlook room while David was laying out the blankets. She just didn't want to deal with other people tonight and typically when the door was locked people didn't bother trying to get in. Ella also made sure she had the commander's key, explaining to him that she needed time to meditate in private on her own to help her manage stress. So, she had the only available key to the lookout.

Ella sat down, tucking her loose skirt under her. Her v-neck, oversized sweater slid off her shoulder, revealing a deep purple strap that held the beginning of lace as it curved over her breast. David held a folded blanket in his lap, hiding how he reacted to her. Then she reached out and took his hand, brought it to her lips to kiss it, and then placed it on the breast that the sweater partially revealed.

David cupped her breast and grazed his thumb over her nipple, feeling her react to his touch. She moved towards him, leaning over in her movement, causing the sweater to gape open and reveal the sheer bra with the edge of lace beneath. Definitely not military issued.

He moved to unbutton his pants as she scraped her hands up his chest under his t-shirt. His shaft sprung from his pants as he released it, ready for her at any moment. She reached for the edge of his pants and pulled them down his legs and off of him. Then she pulled her sweater off, revealing her breasts in the sheer bra, that left her bare and revealed. Her loose skirt draped over the curve of her hips, hiding her center.

As she crawled towards him, she enveloped his shaft into her mouth. Taking him in fully, sucking at him, grazing her teeth along him. As she orally performed for him, he tried his best to hold back, but failed spilling into her mouth. Once done, she kissed the tip of his shaft with a warm smile.

He pulled her to him and cupped her mound, inserting his fingers deftly into her while massaging the pearl that hardened under his touch. She moaned as he lay under her straddled above him. He pushed her hips down on his still hard shaft, guiding her to rub herself along him. As she reached her climax, he delayed it by guiding her up and down onto him. She kept her rhythm, riding him, as he used his thumb to massage her pearl, which caused her to catch her breath with every flick of his thumb. Then slowly she released around him, enveloping him deeply, pushing against him to feel his shaft deep inside her, piercing her completely. Without warning, he spilled into her and she cried out for him to make her his.

David knew he was lost to her forever.

Ella was unsure of what she'd just done.

12

WILDLIFE

Ella and David headed out on a sample retrieval, aiming to see if there were other areas that the algae may be located. They set up the temporary shelter as normal and Ella travelled out to each location as directed by David, who remained located at the central location. The weather looked clear and they planned on making good time and back within the six hours. The last couple of expeditions had cut it too close for their comfort and they wanted to be sure today wasn't the same.

She finished with the last sample and transmitted back to David that she was on her way back. He told her that things looked good and they were making great time. Then she heard a rumbling in the distance.

"David, do you hear that?" She asked.

"No, what are you hearing?" He questioned.

"It sounds like a loud rumble," she answered.

David checked his monitors to see if anything showed up on his scanners. He didn't see any weather developments near them.

"I don't see anything that would be causing thunder

near you. Do you see anything that could be causing it?" David asked.

Ella scanned her area and tried to determine where the noise was coming from. Then she felt the ground vibrating.

"Um, David, can you see things that aren't weather related?" She asked nervously.

"No, why?" He responded.

"The ground is vibrating…"

Then it came out of the stand of trees and charged towards Ella. She couldn't move fast enough before it rammed her and threw her to the side. David saw through her helmet camera the beast charge at her and then saw the vibration as she hit the ground. David started running to Ella, not having any idea what he would do to help her.

When he got to her there was blood running down her face from a head wound he couldn't see. He started to scan the area to be sure the animal wasn't charging back at her, but the area was quiet and still. So, David turned to Ella and began scanning her body.

Her arm was broken and she was unresponsive. David knew he needed to secure her spine and be sure she wasn't moved in any way that would injure her further. He opened the console of her expedition suit and started pressing buttons to make the suit rigid with air pressure. Once the suit was rigid, David lifted her by her armpits and began dragging her back to their temporary shelter.

The travel back took longer than he realized. He realized that they had thirty minutes to get back to Alpha Base Camp. It took them at least an hour to get to this location. David knew they would not make it back with enough oxygen to be able to survive. Additionally, the time continuum would be disrupted, destroying the samples and warping the time of their current time stream. He had to make a quick decision, especially considering Ella's injuries.

He looked on his scanner to see how far they were from the permanent colony. He knew they could provide medical assistance and could then contact Alpha Base Camp to send them assistance for their return. The permanent colony was 15 minutes away. David left everything behind and took Ella in the rover to the permanent colony to receive the medical help she needed.

DAVID DROVE up to the colony gates, which looked like a compound keeping things out. He knew that they were Ella's only chance for survival after the alien animal charged her in the field. He buzzed the door and set the alarms off in the colony. A light shone on him and a metallic voice requested he identify himself and why he was at the colony.

"I'm Major David Catlan with Alpha Base Camp. My fellow scientist, Lieutenant Colonel Ella Jones, was charged by an animal on our expedition. We couldn't make it back to Alpha Base Camp within our six hour window. She is in need of immediate medical attention," David explained.

He heard the alarms buzzing as the doors to the colony opened. A medical team rushed out and took Ella into the colony with David following behind. The leaders took the Rover and drove it into the colony and the doors closed behind them.

13

MEDICAL EVALUATION

Ella lay on the exam table, too still and quiet for David's comfort. He watched as the doctors deflated her suit and opened it to reveal her body. David was afraid of the worst, with her not moving and not being alert. He could see that the right side of her head was covered in blood from the impact of the animal. Her left arm was broken in several places and her left leg was severely swollen. The swelling prevented the doctors from being able to determine the extent of the injuries without x-rays.

They drew blood and sent her blood to their lab. Then they rolled her body to take a CAT scan of her body to determine the damage she underwent, especially if their were internal bleeding. They draped her abdomen to protect her reproductive organs from radiation. They treated her as they would any female patient, not knowing her medical history.

They found her bones severely deteriorated from multiple hairline fractures and areas of her bones that were dying. They had never seen an extensive diagnosis like hers on the planet. They were unsure of how they would help her heal, since multiple compound breaks in this disease resulted in blood loss to her extremities. David sat there, panicking about how he would get Ella back to Alpha Base Camp and tell her husband how she got injured. David didn't even want to talk to Martin, especially after the intimacy he shared with Ella.

The colony leader showed David to temporary housing while Ella stayed in their medical facility. She remained unconscious but stable. Each day, David would come sit with her, then head over to their transmission center and attempt contact with Alpha Base Camp. They were not responding. He was requesting medical support and transportation back to the camp, but was not sure they were receiving his signals.

AFTER TEN DAYS IN A COMA, Ella began slowing responding and waking up. As she opened her eyes, she didn't recognize her surroundings. She took not that her left arm was in a cast with metal rings around it with pins stuck into the cast. She suspected the pins were also connected to her bones and arm, though she was unable to feel or move the arm. Her body felt like a freight train hit it, and she found it difficult to breathe.

Then she saw a movement in the corner of her eye and discovered she couldn't turn her head toward the movement. They had her head stabilized to prevent her from moving it in her sleep. The next moment, David was hovering above her so she could see him without moving her head. She smiled briefly, not sure of what was going on. He placed his hand on her cheek and saw him look at her with tears in his eyes. He then called for the doctors.

They came in and told him to give them a few minutes alone with her. The doctors gave her a run-down of her injuries and the expected healing prognosis. They told her that while most of her injuries and bruising would heal, her arm would more than likely remained damaged and useless. They would manage any pain that she may experience and hopefully over time they would find treatments that could help her.

She was grateful for their honesty and concerned for her prognosis.

"There is one more thing I need to tell you," the doctor stated.

"Okay…" Ella stated, feeling a bit alarmed by the look on the doctor's face.

"We took a blood sample, which is a normal practice for medical treatment, especially in patients that are unresponsive. We ran a panel of tests to determine any underlying diseases or conditions. We discovered that you are pregnant, a few weeks or so."

She just stared at the doctor, wondering how to process the prognosis. "How?"

"Well, typically, a person gets pregnant by having intercourse with a person of the opposite sex. Have you experienced anything of the sort?" The doctor asked clinically.

"My husband and I have been through fertility treatments and we cannot get pregnant," Ella answered.

"Oh, he seems to love you so much. This must be a surprise," the doctor stated with a hopeful smile.

"What?" Ella began to question, "Oh, yes, my husband." She realized that the doctor thought David was her husband. She needed to have David aware of what they thought and were assuming. "Can I see my husband now? I want to tell him the news."

"Of course! We'll bring him right in," the doctor said

rushing out the room. He brought David in and hesitated to leave. Ella motioned with her hand that he could leave and gave him a big happy smile that was unusual for her. This made David aware that something was amiss as the doctor walked out of the room.

"Ella, what are you up to?" He asked seriously.

"They think we are married!" She exclaimed.

"Oh, that may be my fault. They couldn't give you some types of medical treatment unless I was your spouse. So, I told them we were married," David admitted.

"David! You did what?!" Ella fussed.

"You would have died! I couldn't let you die," he stated. He grabbed her uninjured hand and squeezed it.

"Well, there's also another issue. They think we are pregnant," she informed him.

"Now why would you say that to them or make them think that? It's not like you can fake a pregnancy," David stated.

"They did a blood test on me and told me I am a few weeks pregnant," she said.

"But you and Martin couldn't have children, right?" David asked.

"Martin and I were together over three months ago. Then I had the procedure and he left on his geological mission," she said looking at David seriously.

"We met up for drinks the night after he left, right?" David confirmed.

"Yes, we did. Do you think?" She asked him.

David smiled at her warmly and placed his hand on her belly. Then he leaned down and kissed her deeply. "Here in this place, in this time, you shall be my wife. I pledge myself to you."

She smiled back at him, "And I to you."

14

HEALING PROPERTIES

A few weeks later, David and Ella were given quarters in the colony to give her a chance to continue healing. David doted on Ella as she recovered from her injuries. Even her arm was somewhat useful, though she realized she would not make a complete recovery.

At night, David cradled Ella in his arms gently, holding her as if she were fragile and about to break. Ella would lay still listening to his breathing, waiting on the moment his hand would drift down to her belly in his sleep. Even sleeping, he couldn't hide his intense desire to have a child with her.

She felt shame at getting pregnant so easily with David, when she couldn't with her own husband. Then she remembered that the hormone shot Martin insisted on giving her forced her eggs to release, ready to accept David's fertile seed on their drunken night when Martin left her alone. She fell asleep thinking about the encounter where she conceived their child every night as he held her in his arms.

At times David caught her daydreaming with her hand resting on her abdomen. He wondered what she was thinking, wondered if her peaceful appearance indicated something that made her happy. He thought that if fathering a child with her satisfied her, then he could be content.

That morning David went to assess the supplies they had left in the Rover to determine if they had enough to make it safely to Alpha Base Camp. He discovered that they had left too many supplies at the temporary site, and that to go out to the site to gather those supplies, he would deplete the current supplies further and prevent them from returning home.

He came back and informed Ella of the situation. So they planned on transmitting to Alpha Base Camp their situation and the list of supplies they needed in order to return and continue their mission. They determined that they would transmit the list first thing in the morning.

The next morning…

Ella and David headed to the transmission room with their list. The people in the control room told them that the transmission would go through but they had never received a transmission back from Alpha Base Camp. They tried contacting the camp anyway.

"New Colony to Alpha Base," David transmitted.

"This is Alpha Base," a metallic voice came through.

"This is Major David Catlan and Lieutenant Colonel Ella Jones transmitting for supplies," David stated.

"Major Catlan and Lieutenant Colonel Jones have been missing for three months. Please identify the situation," they reported.

"We are not missing. Repeat, we are not missing. There was an accident with a native species. Lieutenant Colonel Jones needed immediate medical assistance in order to survive. We need supplies and have a list," David informed.

"Did Lieutenant Colonel Jones survive the accident?" The voice asked.

"Yes. I'm going to report the supplies we need to return," David said.

"No need. We are not authorized to send supplies," the voice said.

"What? But we need to get back to Alpha Base to continue the mission," David said.

"The mission has been decommissioned and canceled," the voice informed.

"We have only been her for a few weeks. How can it be decommissioned?" Ella asked over the transmission.

"It has been over three months that you have been missing. Your project was cancelled. There is no funding for it." The voice said.

"Then send supplies to get us back to Alpha Base so we can go home," Ella insisted.

"We do not have the authorization to send supplies to New Colony," the voice stated.

"Who are you? Let me speak with your commanding officer!" She insisted. The transmission went silent. She looked at David and started to cry. Ella was not a crying type of person, but her emotions, the stress, her injuries, and her hormones combined hit her all at once. David wrapped her in his arms and hugged her, whispering, "I'm here no matter what happens."

15

LOST IN ACTION

Martin watched as the Military Police approached the door to his and Ella's home. Ava was sitting on their couch with a glass of wine in her hand looking back to see what they said. She knew Martin would tell her what they said. She also knew that David's parents would be informed of anything that happened to him, but they would fail to pass the news on to her, unless it was bad.

Martin opened the door. "Can I help you?"

"Mr. Jones, we regretfully are here to inform you that Lieutenant Colonel Ella Jones has been reported as Missing In Action with her research partner Major David Gordon. They are presumed dead after they went on an expedition in the field. There was an accident with alien wildlife and they were unable to return back to their base camp in time before running out of oxygen. Their bodies were not recovered and are missing after another expedition team went on a search and rescue mission the following day."

Martin stood there stunned at what they were telling

him. He thanked them and gently closed the door. Ava waited for him on the couch. He sat down quietly and sighed heavily. He picked up his wine glass and gulped the contents down, only to pour another glass.

"Martin, how can I help you?" Ava asked.

"I just wish we could have had one last night together. Instead, I went off on a mission and wasted two months of time I could have spent with her," he said as a tear fell down his cheek.

"Again, how can I help you? You wanted to ask me something before the MPs knocked on the door," she stated.

"I was going to ask you to carry my baby. Be our surrogate," he stated with a horrified laugh.

"Okay. I can do that," Ava stated. She was angry that David still had feelings for Ella, though he would never admit it to her. Her best revenge was to be a mother to Ella's child when she wasn't able to carry the child. Even better, Ella wouldn't be there to claim her motherhood when Ava knew she would want rights to any baby she carried.

"Really? Are you sure?" Martin asked.

"Absolutely. Just tell me when the procedure is," she stated.

"Funny you should ask that. There is a way of conception that is a new movement, that mimics natural conception. The hormonal surges are supposed to increase the likelihood of the embryo implantation."

"Oh?"

"Let's get through the memorial services first and then we can talk about it more."

"Martin, do you mind if I stay tonight? I really don't want to be alone. I know David's parents will be insistent on being unwelcoming to me. I don't think I can manage that tonight," she purred.

"I suppose that would be fine. I don't think I can sleep anyway," he answered.

"Me either, so you can tell me about this new way of conceiving, this natural conception idea," she stated scooting towards him.

"Well, let me get the binder to get you all the details about it, so you are comfortable with it," he said.

"Martin, I trust you. We've been intimate before, and all that scientific mumbo jumbo will just go over my head. Why don't you just talk to me about it."

"Well, they will inject you with a shot of hormones the day before the procedure so your uterus is receptive to the embryo. The next day they will set up a procedure, the invitro-fertilization procedure for the egg. Then I will immediately come into the room and penetrate you in intercourse, which causes hormones in your body to release in orgasm to help with the embryo implantation."

She thought it all sounded so clinical and cold. She reached out and touched his cheek, grazing her nails along his stubble. "That seems so unromantic and unhealthy for the best production of those hormones that you need me to produce. Is there a way we could make it less clinical?"

"Well, there are some places that set up a nonclinical location, a place that is more sensual for conception. Usually, those are places for couples to attempt conception. I didn't think you would want that as a surrogate," he stated.

"Oh, Martin, I think that would be a better situation for me. The clinical environment would just feel, embarrassing. I can't do what you need me to do in that setting," she insisted. "In fact, even the sensual setting with doctors around may make me uneasy, especially without acclimating myself to how you feel and move."

"We could practice before hand?" He suggested.

"That sounds like a good plan." She leaned into him and kissed him.

Martin exited the black sedan, wearing his dress uniform. He spotted Ava standing off to the side, not being given a place of honor as David's fiancé. She was being frozen out of a seat in the front by the immediate family. So, he approached her quietly, reached for her hand, and guided her to sit by him, a spouse of one of the fallen astronauts. What he didn't realize was that the press was covering Ella's and David's memorial service, since their research and report of being lost in action was a news headline that impacted the space and research program.

Photographers snapped photos of Martin guiding Ava over to a seat of honor, and he became a headline as the devoted spouse of Ella who had a deep respect for the grieving woman who had planned to marry the other lost astronaut. She sat there beside him with her hands on her lap, gazing at the empty coffins that represented the lost astronauts. A tear drifted down Ava's cheek and Martin had the urge to wipe it away, but he kept his hands down and tried to keep his eyes diverted.

click

When the honor guard lifted their rifles and conducted the three-volley salute, Ava flinched back and Martin placed his hand on her back to steady her. He heard a quiet click of a camera, and thought it was the press documenting the memorial. She leaned in to him, letting him steady her. Then she dropped her head and cried in a beautiful way that would cause other women to become envious and despise her stunning beauty.

click

As the memorial service ended and Ella's flag was handed to Martin and David's flag was handed to his mother, Ava stayed close to Martin. David's family took notice of how familiar she seemed to be with Martin, though she showed no outward signs of intimacy. They did not invite her into their family sedan, so Martin offered to let her ride in his sedan. She had taken an Uber to the service, so accepted his invitation to ride from the memorial in his sedan.

click

He opened the door for her and guided her into the sedan seats, holding her hand and treating her with respect. Then he slid into the sedan seat next to her. *click* The door closed and he instructed the driver to head to his house. Then Martin rolled up the privacy window between the driver and the back of the sedan. He placed his hands on Ava's cheeks and pulled her to him, kissing her deeply.

"Ava, let me console you tonight. Let me help you feel like you are welcome, because you were not treated with respect," Martin insisted. She nodded her head and placed her hand on his chest, melting into his embrace. He ravaged her neck, kissing and nipping at her. She squeezed her thighs together to counteract the heat that pulsed between her legs.

"Not here. The driver may hear," she stated.

"You're right."

The car soon pulled into Martin's driveway. He rolled down the privacy window and handed the driver a hundred dollar bill for his silence and to keep what he may have witnessed or heard private. Little did Martin know, the paparazzi pays more. The driver took the money and drove off leaving Martin and Ava standing at the base of the stairs to his home.

click

Martin took her hand and led her into his home, wrapping his hand around her waist and pulling her into a kiss as he closed the front door.

click

Ava stumbled towards him in desperation to feel comfort and warmth from him. She pushed his uniform jacket off of his shoulders and started unbuttoning his shirt. They stumbled towards the couch, open to the windows overlooking the sea. *click* Martin then lifted Ava into his arms and carried her up the stairs to his and Ella's bedroom.

He unzipped the back of Ava's black lace dress, wondering all day what she had hidden beneath the delicate lace, and slowing pulled it down to the floor. She stood there in black lace lingerie that accentuated her curves. The demi-bra scooped down, barely covering her hard nipples; and the lace of her panties were held together by three thin bands that hugged the curve of her hips and plunged into the cleft of her ass. Martin moaned at the sight of her in her lace, knowing he was ready for her.

click

THE PHOTOGRAPHER FOLLOWED Ava and Martin with his camera as they entered the house. He expected to take photos of them having dinner together and a glass of wine. He was thrilled to discover that they were intimate and having an affair. He became a voyeur as he took photo after photo of Martin undressing Ava, stripping down, and plunging himself into her. To the photographer, they seemed very familiar to each other. He knew he had gotten what he came for, but couldn't leave as he watched them pleasure each other through the night.

Then he sent the photos to his editor, being sure to meet the deadline.

16

PAPARAZZI

Martin got up and headed downstairs to make coffee for Ava and himself. As was his habit, he turned on the news and listened from the kitchen, waiting on the national headlines. What he heard, then saw, took him off guard.

"It turns out a romance may have begun between the the spouse and fiancé of the astronauts lost in action," the anchor stated.

Martin saw a photo of him with his hand on Ava's waist during the memorial service. The photo showed a man looking down at her in complete devotion. Martin questioned if that was himself, because his mind could not process what he was seeing. Then they showed a photo in front of his home, holding Ava's hand and leading her inside. The third photo revealed him kissing her in his living room, a photo that was definitely taken from outside of his property. He was horrified.

"We cannot show any other photos from this tryst, since they are too revealing," the reporter stated. Martin rushed to the windows and closed the blinds, then rushed upstairs and pulled the curtains he was used to having open closed.

"What's wrong?" Ava asked as she started to wake up to Martin rushing around.

"They have pictures of us!" He exclaimed frantically.

"Who? What? What are you talking about?" She asked stretching lazily, revealing herself to him seductively.

"We are all over the news!" He informed her. She grabbed her cell phone to see the news and discovered the tabloid sites were revealing photos of her standing in her lace lingerie with Martin kneeling at her feet, kissing her thigh.

"Well, we are more than on the news," she said as she held up her phone. He sat down on the edge of the bed, horrified that the photo was of them last night in this very bedroom. Horrified that anyone would stalk them and take photos of them in his private home. He went to the shades in the front windows of the house to discover that the road at his driveway was filled with reporters and news vans.

"There are reporters out there."

Well, let's face this head on. We were lonely and our friendship developed over time with Ella and David off on a mission. Last night was a weak moment where we needed comfort instead of being alone. Please give us privacy as we find our own way to mourn together. That's how we will spin this," Ava stated. Martin nodded his head in agreement, knowing that Ava had a way of presenting herself that made people listen.

They got dressed and headed to the front door with cups of coffee. She presented their position to the reporters and the news crews with a warm smile and her stunning beauty. She flirted the nation into adoring them as the two heartbroken spouses that needed someone who could understand what they were feeling. She lured the nation into her web and spun a tale of budding romance that made them famous and adored.

In the next week, Martin and Ava went to the fertility clinic together, since she had agreed to become a surrogate for him and Ella. Reporters followed them and took photos. Again, Ava announced that she had agreed to be a surrogate for Martin and Ella's fertilized eggs. She stated that she couldn't live with herself if Martin never had the chance to father a child with his deceased spouse, and she was happy to help him have their baby with him. This announcement was sealed with a sweet kiss from Martin and he held her hand as they entered into the clinic with flash bulbs lighting their way.

The nurse called her back to the exam room. They took a sample of her blood and gave her a round of hormone shots to help increase her viability for receiving the egg implantation. The procedure consisted of an ultrasound and intrauterine implantation of the viable eggs. They implanted two in her in hopes that at least one would remain viable. She was rolled into the natural conception room, where Martin waited for her.

When the medical staff left the room, he lifted her off the gurney and placed her on the provided bed. Then he proceeded to gently have sex with her. He wasn't supposed to orgasm or make her orgasm, but he was overcome with the idea that she was pregnant with his baby and spilled himself into her.

The next few days, Ava felt the tell-tale signs of sensitivity related to ovulation for her. She knew her hormone levels were higher and she felt increased desire and need. She thought maybe what she was feeling was the implantation of the eggs. So, she went to Martin and lured him seductively into bed. Little did they know, Martin's virility increased with the idea that Ava was pregnant with his child. His increase in fertility combined with her own ovulation caused them to conceive a child of their own, which implanted beside the one of the inseminated eggs from Martin and Ella.

Ava was having twins.

PART 2

PERMANENT COLONY

17

NORMALIZING

Life in the Permanent Colony proved different. Ella and David were tasked with examining the biological samples in the greenhouses. They worked in separate areas, hers in the biological development of food resources, his in the testing of new species for harvesting. They found useful roles that helped the colony prosper.

As the days passed, Ella grew into the fact that they would not be returning to Earth, that no one was coming to rescue them. She also settled into the idea that she would never have to face Martin and tell him she had a baby with David. In fact, she would never see Martin again. So, she resigned herself with an easy and settled life with David and a baby on the way.

David fashioned wedding bands for the two of them to wear out of melted copper and alloys he gathered from discarded equipment in the colony. He made a picnic and retrieved a temporary shelter to put in the rover. He arranged with the colony a day he and Ella could be alone and relieved of their responsibilities for the day. Since she'd been told about the pregnancy, she had been distant from him, making excuses at night to go check on samples. They had not been intimate in weeks, which David knew was a signal that Ella was unhappy with the situation.

He went to her lab to steal her away for the day.

"Hi! I have a surprise for you," David announced.

"I'm not in the mood for any more surprises. I think this baby is enough of a surprise," she stated.

"You have the day off. Come with me," David said. Her supervisor told her to go, that she needed to have a day of rest. It was noted that she worked too much and that it was bad for the pregnancy. Reluctantly, she went with David.

He drove her out to a cliff that overlooked a valley. He spread out a blanket and put out the picnic. Then he set up the temporary shelter. She wondered what he was doing, since a picnic was nice but didn't seem to register as a surprise as significant as he seemed to insist he had. Then she turned around and saw that he was undressing.

"David, what are you doing?" She asked. He was silent as he approached her completely naked. He was stunningly beautiful, with a tall muscular frame that was tanned golden by the alien suns.

"Shh…" he told her as he reached for her clothing and started to unbutton and disrobe her. She stood very still in the light and under his gaze. His hands grazed her shoulders as he brushed her clothing off her. The top half of her body was revealed and he noticed her breasts were fuller and more voluptuous than before. He took them in his hands and lifted them to his mouth, where he kissed and suckled each one, making sure he gave each the same amount of attention. She sighed under his adoration, the area between her legs awakening and throbbing.

Then he wedged his hands under the stretchy waistband of her long skirt and slid it down her thighs, running his hands down her buttocks and legs. He trailed his fingers along the backs of her knees as he knelt down. Then he buried his face in her mound, flicking his tongue out to taste her. She moaned as his tongue traced the path of her sex and darted in and out, increasing her desire. Then he stood up, grazing his body along hers.

He wrapped his left arm around the small of her back and pulled her into him, while he cradled her sex with his right hand and manipulated her desire like the vibrating strings of a guitar. He knew how to bring her to ecstasy. She yelled out against his chest as he brought her up and over the edge of pleasure. Then he kissed her.

"Ella, I love you. You are to be the mother of my child. I have loved you since we were in college together. Yet, I never thought we would end up together like this. I cannot say how happy I am that it is you I am stranded with, that I have to pretend to be your husband. So, today I want to propose that we pretend no more," David stated as he pulled the rings from the picnic items.

"David, did you make these?" She asked.

"Yes. I dedicate myself to you. I promise to be a loving partner, pleasing you as much as you want. I promise to be a loving and supportive father to our children. I promise to cherish and care for you for as long as we are together. I invest myself to be your husband and partner and lover on this day," he stated as he slid the band on her finger.

"David, I promise to be your partner and lover. I promise to be a mother to your children and to care for you while we are together. I invest myself to be your wife, partner, and lover on this day," she stated as she slid the band he made on his finger.

While there was no one there to state they were man and wife, they consummated their union to make it so.

18

RAPID PROGRESSION

Ella went to the lab early in the morning since she had trouble sleeping in her last couple weeks of pregnancy. She liked the quiet of the lab in the morning. No one was there and she could put on classical music to calm her. The baby kicked her ribs and she flinched and took a brief breath to get through the sharp pain. Then she rubbed the side of her belly with pressure to try to convince the little one to shift her position out of Ella's rib cage.

In that moment, it felt like the baby made a somersault and dove into her pelvis. Ella froze in place then felt a warm trickle slide down her thighs. She looked down at her feet to see a pool of clear liquid on the floor. Then the vinegar smell wafted up to her nose and she knew the time had come. Her time had come and she was alone in the lab.

She slowly walked over to grab a towel in the closet and dropped it to the floor. She dragged the towel with her foot across the puddle she'd made on the floor. It took an effort of balancing like a hippopotamus as she wiped up the puddle. Then she looked at the towel and pondered how she would pick it up.

There was absolutely no way she could reach down and pick it up. She was afraid to squat down, since her water had broken and she wanted to make sure her baby was safe. Te problem with being on a colony on an alien planet and being a first time mom was that there were no available child birthing classes to teach her that squatting down would not "pop" her baby out after her water broke. She had quite a number of hours to go before she met her baby.

So Ella left the towel scrunched up on the floor next to the door and out of the walkway. She waddled over to her and David's pod habitat that they were given to prepare for a newborn. When she got there he was just back from a run and was in the shower. She wiggled out of her wet undergarments and kicked them into the clothes hamper. She found the "mommy" undergarments they gave her to prepare for this moment and to wick away the wet trickle that continued as she moved around.

David came out of the shower surprised to see her there, since she'd gone into the lab. She had a strange look on her face. He walked over and wrapped his long arms around her and kissed her on the cheek from behind. Then she tensed and clawed her hands into his arms and moaned out loud.

"Whoa. Babe are you hurting?" He asked, knowing their due date had not yet arrived.

"I think it is time. My water broke," she stated, gritting her teeth through a contraction.

"I'll call the doctor, just to check you out and make sure you are okay," he said as he guided her to sit on their couch where she'd laid out a towel.

The doctor came in just as Ella was starting another

contraction. David held up three fingers to let him know that the contractions were three minutes apart. The doctor checked her internally to determine how effaced and dilated she was. Her cervix was 75% effaced and she was 4 centimeters dilated.

"Ella, I can feel the baby's head. I'm not sure if it is the best thing to move you across the colony. How do you feel about giving birth right here?" The doctor asked.

"That's not what we agreed on," she said.

"Well, if you walk across that field, you baby may be born in that field. I have no idea how fast you will give birth. Have you been feeling contractions at all?" He asked.

"I couldn't sleep last night, so I walked into the lab. Nothing unusual — until I left a puddle on the floor!" She exclaimed. The doctor chuckled a bit at her phrasing.

"Okay, but I'm going to radio a couple nurses to bring supplies here and a gurney in case we need anything immediate. I'd rather keep you here where you are safe and in a clean environment," he explained. She reluctantly agreed and lay on the bed.

The evening calmed down a little as she began relaxing into a regular pattern of contractions followed by rest. Then around midnight the intensity of labor increased and she felt the urge to push. Within thirty minutes she and David had a baby girl whom they named Lillian Rose.

As Lillian Rose grew up into a toddler, Ella found it more difficult to lift her with her damaged arm. No amount of physical therapy would relieve the weakness and pain Ella experienced with trying to provide comfort to her young daughter.

Due to this, David began researching biological remedies to create pain medicine developed from planetary resources. He recently found a new resource and wanted to test its effects. He went to her doctors to discuss with them ways to test the new medicinal treatment.

Her doctors had a simulated program that would test the impact of new treatments on the human body. They took various samples of the treatment David created and measured multiple strengths of the drug and its impact. They discovered that the threshold of the treatment resulted in a chemotherapy-like effect or no impact at all on the human body. David took the results to Ella to discuss the side effects of the new treatment.

Ella listened quietly to David as he explained the side effects versus the impact of the treatment to her. She agreed to take the treatment, knowing how much David worked on creating a treatment. She viewed his work as a complete act of love.

"David, before I start the treatment, let's have a few days together alone. I want to make sure that we have time together that is sacred and intimate before this treatment begins."

He agreed to her request and they arranged time away with a close acquaintance to care for Lillian Rose. Ella and David packed up the rover and headed to the cliff they married on. What Ella didn't know was that David had built a house with some of the other colonists to surprise Ella with for their anniversary. When she saw the house, she began to cry.

He reached for her hand to help her out of the rover. She reached for him with her right hand, barely able to grasp it and stepped from the vehicle. They walked toward the stairs of the house and he opened the door for her. As she stepped over the threshold, she looked up to the ceiling that let the light of the sky shine in. He had built clear panels of impact-proof glass into the roof to allow them to read by natural light and to see the stars as they spent their evenings together.

She walked further in to the home and noticed that he had built her a wall of glass that exited onto a porch that overlooked the valley below. There were two bedrooms off to the right side of the house that had two single beds in each, and then she saw the bedroom that would be theirs opened up to the living quarters and attached to the porch overlooking the valley. There was a wall of windows in the room and duplicate ceiling panels, so they could sleep under the stars. The simple kitchen was open to the living area, but was efficient enough to allow them to be independent of the colony.

"David, this is so beautiful," Ella stated in awe.

"I wanted us to have something like what I dreamed we would have back home," he told her.

"But we were with other people on Earth."

"Ella, this is the home I envisioned we would live in when we were in graduate school together. I drew up plans for this home over ten years ago based on the dream home you described to me," David explained.

"What? You created this house then?" Ella looked at him in astonishment, not realizing the depth of love he had felt for her for as long as he did.

"Yes. I had planned on proposing marriage to you with the drafted house plans when we graduated. We were so good together. Then you met Martin our final semester and everything between us ended," David confessed.

"Is that why you told me you needed time alone?" She asked.

"Yes. I couldn't stand to see you with Martin. It hurt so much," David explained.

"Come here. I need you to know that I love you here and now. This is our home together. This is where we will raise Lillian Rose and her baby brother or sister," Ella told him. He looked at her trying to process what she'd just said to him.

"What?" He asked.

"You heard me right. I'm having another baby. We are having another baby. It's why I needed these few days away with you — to tell you I am pregnant, especially in light of the treatment."

"You can't take the treatment if you are pregnant. It is like chemotherapy. It could kill the baby," he said.

"Then I will wait. I won't let anything kill our baby," she told him as she reached for him with her right hand and pulled him to her.

"Let's christen this house," he said.

"I suggest we christen every room."

"Um, not the kids' rooms." He said with a chuckle as he stripped down and lifted her in his arms.

David was hard under her as she straddled him and slowing empaled him into her. She rocked her hips, creating a slow friction between them, and feeling his full length inside of her. He held her hips, pushing them down onto him with added force, knowing in this home she was his wife and she had his heart. In the multiple thrusts her muscles contracted in pleasure around him and she yelled out, something he hadn't heard since their last encounter on Earth since privacy wasn't exactly easy to come by in the colony.

He flipped her over and took her from behind, making sure she felt him fully and completely as he came. Then they lay there under the stars in the living room, gazing up and dreaming of their future together in shared whispers.

Ella felt completely happy and elated in their home

with David, knowing her future was settled and she was content.

Nine months later, she gave birth to Eliza and Jared. With David and being at ease, Ella was able to conceive easily — a feat she was never able to achieve with Martin.

MARTIN AND AVA

Ava and Martin were invited to a celebration of life a month after the memorial service for Ella and David. Ava stretched lazily in the bed, knowing that they had to present themselves perfectly that evening. Martin had bought her a beaded royal blue gown for the ceremony that draped to the floor and was slit up her right leg drastically. The matching stiletto heels caused her to tower almost to his 6'4" height, as her thin, but curvy frame began filling out with the pregnancy.

She bathed in candlelight awaiting Martin to arrive home, hoping they could have an intimate moment together before heading to the ceremony. She heard him arrive home and called him up to her. He walked in his bathroom, and saw Ava bathing seductively. She smiled like a cat with a bowl of cream at him. He undressed and entered the bathtub with her.

Laying in the bath behind her, he grabbed her mound, manipulating it and giving her pleasure. Between her moans, he suggested that she change a few things about her appearance that would please him. He wanted her to grow her hair out and dye it a copper red — the same color hair that Ella had. In fact, he'd hired a stylist to arrive that evening before the ceremony to attend to her hair and suggested she make that change immediately. She agreed and then felt him shift and thrust into her as she sat in his lap. Together they orgasmed and then the doorbell rang.

The stylist came in, ready to make the necessary changes to Ava's hair that would please Martin.

Ava looked at herself in the mirror as the stylist dried her shoulder length hair. Martin came over and murmured something to the stylist, who then reached in her supplies and emerged with hair extensions. In the next hour, Ava was transformed from a brunette with a straight modern bob, to a redhead with long waves of hair streaming down her back. She had never imagined herself in this way, and felt a moment of lost identity as she looked in the mirror at the change.

The stylist left, looking at Ava forlornly knowing that the change did not make her client happy. Martin brought out the royal blue gown and draped it on the bed. Ava began getting dressed and ready for the ceremony.

"You need to change those. I really don't like that. Here, wear this instead," Martin said as he handed Ava a set of lingerie that he'd stored in a drawer. She wondered where he had gotten it from.

"Martin, I've never worn anything like these. They may be difficult with the dress," Ava stated.

"Make it work. I plan to sneak off at some point during the dinner with you," he stated frankly.

Ava was somewhat embarrassed about his plan, but at

the same time aroused at the excitement. She adorned herself with the corset that was boned with metal and laced in the back at her waist. Her breasts had swollen and were bursting out of the corset, barely covering her nipples. The panties, she discovered, were a sheer lace thong that barely covered her but would not leave lines under the gown. As she walked, the delicate lace rubbed her and caused arousal with their friction. She wondered how she would make it through the evening.

She adorned her body with the gown, which was noticeable snug around her breasts and abdomen. She had not realized the changes in her body and how her pregnancy was changing the shape of her thin form. Hopefully, the photographers would not notice the change in her body. She entered into the living room where Martin waited. He turned to her and smiled. Then he approached her, kissed her, and reached under the slit of he dress to graze his finger along her cleft. She jolted at his touch knowing she would want him whenever he called.

They headed to the ceremony and exited the limousine. Photographers and reporters were waiting at the event, ready to take permanent images to document the event. Martin helped Ava out of the limo as the slit in her dress shifted, almost revealing her to the cameras flashing as she made sure her thighs pressed together upon emerging. The flashes caught the flaming hair upon her head, reporters taking note of her transformation and how similar she looked to Martin's late wife, Ella. The beads reflected in the cameras along every curve of Ava's body, accentuating her swollen bosom and expanding abdomen.

Halfway through the formal event, Martin suggested they take a walk to escape the stifling crowd. He made excuses that they needed a moment since the event was emotional. All around were so understanding and expressed their sorrow for the two.

Escaping the ballroom, Martin led Ava down a corridor and into a room with a chaise and couch with long windows overlooking the river. He locked the door behind him and led Ava over to the windows. Deftly, he unzipped her dress and it fell to the floor. He kicked it away and turned her toward him. Her breasts burst from the corset as he lifted her arms over her head and held her wrists against the wall. He reached between her legs, feeling how ready she was for him, and pulled himself free from his tuxedo pants. Then he had her wrap her legs around his waist and pressed her against the frame of the windows, thrusting himself inside of her until they released with pleasure. *click* This was the most exciting part of the event and Ava looked forward to returning with a secret only they shared.

The papers and news the next day reported on the couple and how their sorrow of lost love brought them together. The tabloids decided to take a different approach. They gathered images of Ella from the inauguration event of the astronauts and their mission to the planet. In the images, she wore a royal blue dress and her long auburn hair in waves down her back. Ava's image from the event, which she'd attended with her former fiancé was placed beside Ella's to show the differences in the two women. Then the new photo's of Ava were presented as the changes she'd made in order to look like Ella — the red hair and royal blue gown. They suggested she had lured Ella's husband into her web, naming her the "Spider Whore." What Ava missed was the images on the next page that showed them copulating in front of windows overlooking the river, while the formal event continued elsewhere.

Ava was horrified by the reports. She was further disturbed by the highlights of the curves in her body. She noticed the changes and how tight her dress was. She wondered how long she had until she couldn't hide her pregnancy, noticing that she was showing a lot sooner than she expected.

Martin entered the room and handed her a coffee. He sat down beside her and saw the tabloid reports, then chuckled. "Oh, you are now famous. We are famous! But I must say, I like the idea of you being my whore and I really love the web you wove for me," he stated as he fondled the newly red hair. She grimaced as she looked away from him, hating that her hair was red and not realizing that the royal blue dress she'd worn was a dress that Ella would have worn.

He untied her robe and pulled it down her shoulders. He fondled her breasts and urged her onto her knees. She braced her arms on the edge of the couch as he plunged into her vigorously, thrusting and calling her his little spider whore. She was humiliated and cried when he left for work, leaving her naked and raw in his home.

20

TREATMENT

Ella started the treatment a few months after giving birth. Her pregnancy had delayed the treatment, resulting in the progression of her disease. She no longer had use of her left arm and had to wear it in a permanent brace. She only had the use of her right hand, and at times her hand would be numb after prolonged periods of work.

David set up her treatment in their home, so she would be comfortable and in her own environment. He knew the hospital setting would be uncomfortable and that their children would not be allowed to visit her. So he determined that she should receive the treatments and care in their home with the assistance of medical support to help with when the treatment had its full impact.

Ella finished her first treatment and felt queasy from the infusion of biological poison into her blood stream. She decided her best option was to rest and enjoy the porch overlooking the valley that David had built for her. She sat on the deck, drinking water as Lillian Rose ran around playing with her handmade doll. Eliza and Jared were being cared for by their nurse and they were down for a nap.

Ella felt at peace as she sat in the alien light. Then a deep ache in her bones developed slowly. It felt like needles were searing her from inside out and she tensed.

"Lillian, go find Jean," she ordered. "Mommy needs to talk to her about a surprise for you!" Lillian Rose ran off and once out of earshot, Ella wailed out in pain. She shook from the pain. She struggled up out of her chair and hobbled inside to get the pain medication that David brought her. Jean came rushing out to her and helped her inside to the couch.

Ella balled up from the pain. She begged for David. In thirty minutes and after a call from Jean, David arrived home and came to Ella's side. By that point she was throwing up from the pain. David sat with her and brushed her hair from her face. As he pulled her hair back, he noticed white streaks forming down portions of her hair. The poison was changing her genetic and chemical composition. He decided he needed to take a blood sample from her and call her doctors and the researchers from his lab to bring equipment for monitoring to the house.

The doctors arrived and began taking blood samples to test. They found that around twenty-five percent of her cells were changing structure. They had viral attachments to them, looking like they were being attacked and strangled with tendrils wrapping around each cell. David was horrified by what he saw as she endured the pain and kept vomiting. Eventually, Ella passed out from exhaustion, but still flinched from the intensity of the poison in her bloodstream.

Her doctors decided they needed to dose her with morphine to manage the pain and allow her some form of rest. The morphine numbed her pain, yet also reacted to the viral composition of the treatment like giving sugar to yeast. In her sleep, David noticed her left hand twitching, so he took off her brace. Her arm had turned an ugly shade of purple with green undertones. A vine-like pattern of black vessels spread over her arm, looking like her limb was in the process of being strangled and dying. David's heart clenched in his chest trying to understand what he had done to the woman who he loved and pledge himself to — the woman who'd pledged herself as his wife on this planet.

DAYS PASSED and Ella's condition worsened. She insisted on continuing the treatment, since the experimental design showed that the treatment would kill her if she did not receive the complete six rounds. Each week her arm became worse and the viral pattern expanded. She began to lose feeling in her left leg, though she could carefully walk with a cane.

Due to the debilitating effects, David attempted to keep Ella home to be monitored. She refused. Instead, she went into her lab to keep a moderate schedule and feel normal. The children were being cared for by Jean, whom they hired on full time.

Ella secretly began experimenting with extended fuel sources for the rover. She made alternate plans to return to Earth to get medical care, with the intent on returning to the planet once healed. She began making progress on the fuel and realized that the rover would burn away the fuel she created in a matter of an hour. So, she decided once her treatment was complete she would plan an expedition to find new fuel sources.

The sixth treatment was complete. Ella's hair was

completely white. Her left arm was useless and her right hand was permanently numb. She had to wear a brace on her left leg in order to put pressure on it and prevent the bones in it from shattering. The treatment was a failure and David knew it.

He went back to his lab to find a new treatment to heal her. She went back to her lab to test new fuel sources based on biological life on the planet. She sent out an expedition team to collect samples and tested each sample when they returned. Eventually, they found the right plant composition and Ella began making fuel and storing it in tanks.

One night, when she had almost all of the fuel tanks collected, David came home optimistic.

"Ella, I think I found a new treatment. The computer simulation has been reprogrammed to determine how it will specifically react to your genetic composition. I want to show it to you," David insisted. Ella agreed to look at his research, hoping if it were a solution she wouldn't feel the need to go back to Earth for medical help.

What she saw was distressing. The new treatment would need to be given to her over three weeks with three treatments a week. The prospect would be that they would surgically fuse her bones to rods and the infusion of chemicals would reawaken her nerve centers so she would regain the use of her hands. She would have to undergo the surgery first, then remain in the hospital over the course of those three weeks with the treatments given while she is placed in a temporary coma. They couldn't risk an adverse affect of pain meds, like morphine, causing the treatment to mutate or react in an unexpected way.

Ella agreed to undergo the treatment and suggested they spend a quiet and intimate evening together. They had Jean take the children to their former home in the colony so they could have privacy. David attended to Ella's needs and desires, while being gentle in order not to cause damage. While she felt pleasure, her disease drastically impacted their lovemaking and decreased their intimacy.

The next day, when David headed to his lab to prepare her doctors for the upcoming treatment, Ella began writing letters to David and their children. She didn't have the ability to face them and say goodbye. She packed a small satchel and headed to her lab. She told her lab assistants that she was going to test the range of the fuel on the rover that day. She told them that she would be gone for a few hours and then back just before the end of the day. She grabbed copies of her medical files that showed the treatments she had undergone and headed out.

21

ALPHA BASE CAMP

Ella approached Alpha Base Camp after three hours of navigating the terrain. As she approached something seemed different. She entered into the camp and limped into the headquarters. The usually busy room of instrument controllers and personnel was silent and still.

She decided to head toward where the navigation and wormhole generator were located. There were a few people in the rooms and she entered in. They didn't notice that she had entered and continued a transmission to Earth.

"Excuse me," she said. They turned to her and stared at the woman with white hair streaked with copper red. They thought she looked familiar but couldn't place her. They wondered where she came from.

"How did you get here? Who are you?" The first technician said.

"I'm Lieutenant Colonel Ella Jones. I am part of the mission that was retrieving samples to determine the safety of this planet's resources. I need to go back to Earth to report on my findings," she announced.

"Colonel Jones and Major Gordon were reported MIA three months ago. Due to their accident, the program was defunded and shut down. We are here to wrap things up and decommission this site," they told her.

"You can't shut this site down. There is a colony out there that relies on the supplies from this wormhole. Shutting the base camp down will strand them on this planet. You can't do that!" Ella exclaimed.

"We have our orders. But who did you say you are?" He asked her again.

"Colonel Jones. I am Colonel Jones. I need to return home to report on my findings."

They found an image of her and held it up to her face. Then she showed them her identification and her dogtags with her military number on them. They began a transmission back to Earth explaining the situation. Immediately a pod was prepared and she was sent back through the wormhole. The travel was brutal. She passed out from the pain and arrived unconscious to Earth.

Ella remained unconscious for a month. In that time, doctors scanned her body for viruses and contamination and put her in mandatory isolation. They were unsure if she would wake up or remain unconscious. At the end of the month the doctors decided that they needed to contact her husband, Martin Jones to explain the situation. They needed him to decide on what measures they should take to care for Ella.

When Martin received the call, Ava was sleeping soundly in his bed. She was so beautiful and her full belly curved sensually out from her hips. He couldn't resist her as she grew his baby inside of her. At times he imagined she were Ella as he fucked her from behind. Her newly red hair and swollen breasts made it easier for him to imagine her as Ella.

Now he had received a call stating his wife was in a hospital unconscious. His heart sunk thinking that the fun he'd had with Ava was coming to an end. He rushed out the door to head to the hospital. As he drove he wondered how he would break the news that Ava was pregnant with their child, that he had allowed her to be their surrogate. He also wondered how he would tell Ava that Ella had returned and she would need to move out. How would he manage her after telling her they would need to end their interactions?

Martin pondered this, trying to determine a plan of action. The mere thought of Ava aroused him. She let him do things to her that Ella never agreed to or allowed. They had a special relationship where he could go to his dark places and be brutal with her, taking it as he gave it. She never protested or asked him to stop. He'd never taken her to a place where she stated she needed him to stop. Instead, she seemed insatiable — always wanting more from him.

How could he give that up for a wife who seemed reserved and cold towards him? How could he give up intense passion with a woman pregnant with his child for a woman who resisted having a child with him? Martin was torn between duty and desire — between what was socially expected and breaking all the norms of the world.

He arrived at the military hospital and was directed to the Intensive Care Unit on the sixth floor. He showed his identification and was led to room 601. She lay there peacefully, her red hair braided as usual and hanging off the edge of the bed. She looked so fresh and healthy, almost young and vibrant as she slept soundly. Her hospital gown draped loosely over her as he approached. The air conditioner cut on and blew air on her. Her body reacted to the cooler air as he noticed the hair on her arms getting goosebumps.

He reached for the blanket to cover her up and his hand brushed her breast accidentally. His arousal for her was immediate and he felt love for the wife he'd lost a few months ago. He leaned over and kissed her, wondering if she were like Sleeping Beauty from the fairy tales. In her sleep her lips responded to his briefly, but she remained unconscious.

He sat down and talked with her about his research. He told her how they were going to have a baby and that they had a wonderful surrogate. He confessed to her that he'd been having an affair with Ava, but that he had wished she had been Ella many nights they were together. Ella didn't wake up.

That evening her doctors came to her room on their rounds. They explained to Martin that she seemed to be in a lot of pain. They told him that every time they attempted to decrease her pain meds so she could more easily come out of her coma, her body would go into shock, her heart rate would speed up to dangerous levels, and her oxygen intake would drop. They explained to Martin that he needed to decide if they should keep her sedated or try to decrease her medications. They told him that there was the risk that she could have a heart attack and whether he wanted them to take measures to restart her heart if it stopped. They told him her oxygen could also decrease and that she may need to be intubated, but that he needed to decide if they should take those measures. Martin decided that they needed to decrease her medications to get her out of a coma and take all measures necessary to save her life.

THE NEXT MORNING the doctors began to decrease her pain medications. Martin stayed with her through the night, confessing to her all the things he had done that could hurt her. He didn't want her to die without him telling her the truth about everything, even if she couldn't hear him.

He stayed by her side, holding her hand, as the medications slowly decreased. Her heart rate remained stable and her oxygen levels remained normal. By midday, all medications had ceased. Ella remained asleep.

Martin began wondering if she would ever wake up. He was tired and left his phone number with the nurses as he went to grab a coffee. At the coffee stand he ordered two coffees. He decided he would bring his wife a coffee like he did every morning before she left on her mission. Something needed to feel normal for him.

The nurses watched Martin in pity as he walked back to Ella's room with two cups of coffee. He announced to Ella that he brought her a coffee for when she woke up. Her heart rate spiked in response. He noticed. Then he wondered if his normal way of waking her up may work this time to bring her out of her coma. He walked over and pulled the privacy curtain closed. There were mornings where the only way he could wake her from a dead sleep was with sexual fondling and foreplay.

Martin was hesitant at first, but then unsnapped the side of Ella's hospital gown. He kissed her lips then nibbled her neck as he ran his hand across her flat belly that was tight and firm. Her breathing became shallow and her heart rate fluttered.

The nurses came rushing in to find Martin caressing and kissing his wife. They slowly backed away not knowing what to do, especially since she was responding. They were half in pity that this could be just a physical reaction that was biological and that it gave him hope, but at the same time they needed to be sure he didn't violate her. Then they saw her hand move and a smile come across her lips. It looked like she was waking up.

Martin continued to caress her and cupped her full breast in his hands. He'd forgotten how firm her breasts were and how they always filled out her clothes giving her curves that defied the laws of physics on her lean body. He couldn't resist to suckle at her nipple, that called to him as it tightened in reaction to his touch. What he didn't know was that Ella was gazing down at the man giving her pleasure, remembering his familiar ways of waking her up from sleeping. She let him continue to try waking her up as she played possum during his caresses.

He slowly reached down between her legs, caressing the soft curls. He navigated his fingers between her lips to find the flower bud that he could manipulate to make her moan. She was still quiet and still, but her body was responding to his manipulations. He desired to taste her one last time if she were never going to wake up again, so he trailed kisses down her stomach and licked her bud with a flick of his tongue.

David, in all their time together, never savored her like Martin did. David never tasted her, sucked on her, or plunged his tongue into her. She was always satisfied by David, but never savored. She missed this and gasped when Martin's tongue flicked against her. Then she grabbed his hair and spread her thighs for his to have access to her.

She was awake. Martin was so elated and aroused at

the same time that he continued his efforts without a care for the possible medical staff that could walk in. He buried his face in her, plunged his tongue inside of her, and sucked and licked her until she moaned out in desire. Then he mounted her like a stallion rutting.

He thrust into her over and over, reclaiming her and making her his. She met him with every thrust and cried out in pleasure as he continued his movement in a steady rhythm with her. He held back his orgasm, giving her the chance to lose herself in him, allowing her to wrap her body in passion around him. She started shaking and trembling from the waves of pleasure coming over her, as she heightened to a climax unlike any she'd felt in many years. He felt the intense tightening and spilled into her with a few final hard thrusts.

As she panted from exhaustion, he lay on top of her, still nestled inside of her throbbing, making sure every bit of him released into her. Then he pulled out, and bent down to taste her fully, their passion intermingled on his tongue, and came back up to kiss her and let her remember how they tasted together. She threaded her fingers into his hair as she kissed him back deeply, knowing she was home with her husband that could provide her with pleasure unlike any she'd ever known.

Martin lets her know he thought she was lost forever to him.

22

ARRANGEMENTS MADE

It was the sixth month anniversary of Ella and David's memorials. Martin had to leave Ella at the hospital while the doctors checked her out before releasing her. Martin also had to prepare an alternate arrangement for Ava, since she definitely couldn't live in his and Ella's home. This was the house Ella had picked out and they had bought together. This was Ella's dream home on the ocean, the place where they had spent nights naked under the stars merging their bodies together.

He walked up the stairs of the entrance, wondering how he was going to explain the situation to Ava. Slowly he walked into the house.

"Martin, you're home! Where have you been? I was texting you all night and was worried," Ava announced as she approached him to welcome him home with a kiss. He deflected her by turning to hang his jacket up and walked to pour himself a whiskey. Then he sat on the couch quietly.

"Ava, we have to talk," Martin stated. Ava flinched.

This was how breakups started. He was about to breakup with her when she was six months pregnant. She slowly sat down, allowing her robe the fall open and turned to face him with one leg on the couch and the other foot at the floor. She wanted to send him the message that she was sexually ready for him at any point, especially if that could save her connection to him.

"Okay?" She said demurely. He sighed, realizing that even after intimacy with Ella, he still desired Ava sexually and was aroused. Ava glanced down noticing his arousal and smiled expectantly.

"I have to tell you something that is unexpected," he said.

"I do too," she said. He looked at her strangely. "Should I go first?"

"Um, yeah, sure," he said. She leaned over to him and reached for his hands. He stiffened. Then she placed his hands on her belly and smiled.

"We are having two babies. I'm having twins!" She announced to him. His arousal intensified with her news. He imagined the babies he and Ella conceived growing inside of Ava. Before he knew it, Ava was kissing him and reaching for his pants, freeing his shaft. He groaned and she plunged herself around him, rocking on top of him as he held her round belly.

"Ava, stop, please stop," he begged. She stilled her motions and looked at him strangely. Never had he asked her to stop. He then gently moved her away from him and covered himself.

"What's going on? You are acting weird," she stated.

"Ella came through the wormhole. She isn't dead," Martin tole her. Ava clenched at those words. Her emotions welled up and she started crying uncontrollably.

"So, what do we do? She rejected you before she left," Ava stated.

"I don't think she did. I think her feeling were just hurt. She seems different now," Martin expressed.

"So, she is moving back in here? With us?" Ava asked in shock.

"No, not with us. With me, " he said directly.

"Where will I go? I gave up my apartment!"

"I've gotten you a hotel suite to stay in until I can find you an apartment."

"What? Like a whore?"

"No, like the surrogate of my babies."

"That's all I am now? The surrogate?"

"My wife is back. That's all you can be now."

"She won't let you do what you do with me. You will miss it. You will miss me."

"Maybe, but I have to try to make this work, especially with the babies coming."

"How are you going to tell her that I am the surrogate? How are you going to hide all the reports of our passionate affair? It's was all over the news when we were discovered. Don't you think this will be reported on?"

"Probably. I will explain it to her. I have to give it a go with her." Ava stormed upstairs and began packing her clothes and toiletries. She came down the stairs and dialed her cell phone. She was calling an Uber.

"Where is the hotel?" She demanded.

"I'll take you. I have to give them my cell phone anyway," Martin told her. She hung up on the Uber driver and cancelled the transport. Martin drove her to the high end hotel and paid for the room. He told them to charge whatever she needed to his card and to email him her expenses each day.

She walked away with her key to the elevator and refused to acknowledge his attempt at a goodbye. He watched as she disappeared behind the closing doors. Then he left for the hospital to see his wife.

23

HEALTH AND VITALITY

Ella's doctors pulled up the last medical files she had on Earth and compared them to the medical files she had on the planet. They looked at the dates and questioned her about the time differences. She confirmed that a total of seven years had passed while she was on the planet and in the colony. She also told them that David was alive and well.

The questioned her about how her scans there were so different from the scans she had on the planet. She was confused, then it dawned on her that she had the use of her left arm, no longer wore a brace on her leg, and had tactile feeling in her right hand. Her skin was also a normal color that looked very healthy, instead of the grey dead color with black veins from the treatment David had created for her.

She got up from the hospital bed and disrobed, not caring what the doctors saw. She was fully healed and had no outward signs of the disease. In fact, her skin and body looked like it had regenerated, because she no longer had the stretch marks she'd become accustomed to seeing everyday spreading like a terrain map across her abdomen. Her body looked the same age as it had been before going to the planet. She was looking at the long lost body of the woman she used to know — a woman at her prime.

"Once I report and make my recommendations, I will need to return to the planet," she stated thinking of her children and David as she put her hospital gown back on. Then she felt horrible. She'd had intercourse with Martin. She was in a predicament. She would need to explain the situation and years of companionship to Martin, only to leave him. Then she would need to confess to David not only why she left, but also that she had reunited with her husband momentarily without thought.

"Colonel Jones, you can't go back through the wormhole," the General standing at the door stated.

"Why? We need to get supplies back to the Colony. They need our support," Ella demanded, thinking of what would happen to her children if supplies were not procured.

"The wormhole collapsed," he stated flatly then saw the devastated look that came across her face. "I'm so sorry."

"What will happen to the people there?" She asked.

"They will either figure out a way to survive and harvest food in the years it will take to send a team with supplies to them, or the team will find remains of the colony. It is an awful situation," he stated.

"What happened to the wormhole?" She asked.

"We don't know. We are trying to see if it comes back after a solar storm ends. But that solar storm is supposed to last for three months."

"That is at least seven years there. What will the solar storm do to the planet?" She asked.

"That's what we need your scientific expertise on. We

need help taking measurements and determine if you see any changes in the planet's atmosphere. We need to know what to expect when our astronauts arrive," he said. She shook her head, hoping that whatever knowledge she could provide to the program would help keep her children and David alive.

A COUPLE HOURS later Martin arrived at the hospital to pick Ella up and take her home. They drove down the coast of the Monterey Bay with his top down, so Ella could feel the sea air on her face. Tendrils of her auburn hair flowed from her braid and floated around her face. He pulled into their driveway and Ella looked at their home. It felt eerily familiar in some way.

She walked in with Martin and looked up at the ceiling, only to be disappointed at not seeing clear panels letting the light into the room. The layout of the first floor was very familiar to the layout of the home David had built her on the alien planet. She had always considered this home to be the dream home she had described to David in grad school.

"Martin, do you remember who we bought this house from?" She asked.

"I had the house built. David gave me these plans he'd drafted and told me this would be your dream home. He told me it was a secret wedding gift," Martin explained.

"Oh," Ella said as she slowly sat on the couch and wondered if she would be able to live in the home and not see images of her children running around haunting her.

"Hey, are you feeling okay?" Martin asked as he noticed she sat down and was in a strange mood.

"Yeah, just need to go sit on the deck," she said. Martin led her to the deck and brought her blanket to her.

"I'll get you a coffee," he said as he went back in and scanned the room for any missing items his cleaning lady had missed. As he started the coffee he bolted up the stairs to be sure the bedroom and master bath was all in order and cleared of any of Ava's items. His cleaning lady had done a spectacular job at making the evidence of Ava disappear.

Martin rushed back down and made Ella's coffee. Then he brought it to her. She quietly accepted it and smiled at him briefly.

"So, I know we didn't part on pleasant terms when I left on my mission and left you here alone for the final month back home. I feel horrible about that. But when they pronounced you dead, I felt very alone…" Martin started. Ella looked over at him wondering where this confession was going.

"You do know we tried to get back, right?" Ella asked.

"We?" Martin questioned.

"Yes, David and me. After he had to take me to the colony to save my life, because I was going to die from the accident and we couldn't make it back to the Camp, we contacted Alpha Base to get home. They refused to send supplies or fuel. Then they stopped all communication signals to the colony," Ella told him.

"What? They abandoned you?" Martin questioned.

"Yes."

"Then what I am about to tell you makes me feel worse," he said.

"Whatever it is, I will try to understand. You thought I was dead. They told you I was dead," she stated and touched his hand.

"I had an affair with Ava. She and I were so lonely. I

had already proposed that she serve as the surrogate to our child, the last part of you I had. She will have our twins in three months," he told her.

"Where is she now?" Ella asked.

"In a nice hotel suite. I thought that would be best for her until the babies were born," he stated.

"I agree. How are David's parents reacting to this?" She asked.

"His parents refused to acknowledge her at the memorial service for you and David. So, I had her sit with me and ride from the memorial service with me. You may see photos of us together, and some not so flattering," he said.

"Really? How bad?" She asked.

"Well…Some photos are revealing. Some were taken of us upstairs from outside. Others at a party just a before you came back from the planet and they told me you were back," he confessed.

"So, do you think they are stalking us now? Wondering how your wife returned will interact with you?" She asked.

"Probably," he said.

"Then let's give them a show," she said with a smile. She needed to feel better about the seven years she'd had with David. She needed to feel better about never being able to return and abandoning them to a life without her, possibly death now. She needed to become the wife Martin needed and the future mother to the two children Ava was bringing into the world. She also needed to erase Ava from his mind.

Martin kissed her. As they kissed, she unbuttoned and opened up her clothing to reveal herself to him and the elements of the sun and beach air. He pushed all her clothes off of her.

click

She lay on the deck chair with his face buried in her

mound as she reached her arms over her head to reveal her breasts to the sky.

click

Martin disrobed and stood straddling her with his manhood at her face. He grabbed her hair and led her to him. She enveloped him in her mouth and wrapped her arms around his rear, clawing at his buttocks as he pushed himself into her.

click

Right before he came he pulled her away, turned her around, and took her from behind on the deck chair. She held onto the back of the chair as he slammed into her with force, remolding her to him. She needed the remaking, to feel different with him, to not be treated gently like David had treated her. She desired to have Martin become rough with her, to make sex different and primal. With the last few thrusts he came and pulsed his seed into her.

click

He reached around and massaged her cleft, manipulating her to orgasm and spasm around him. As she did, he became aroused again and began moving in and out as he massaged her and led her to another climax. In the strongest climax she had he pounded into her and took advantage of how sensitive and responsive her body was to him. He orgasmed again, burying himself deeper into her, pulsing his seed deep into her womanhood. Something about her felt different to him, and he liked it.

THE PAPERS the next day reported on the reunion of husband and wife. The tabloids printed photos of their sexual escapade on the deck and how they seemed to have a deeper connection with the reunion. The cold distant nature they reported that Ella had before her mission was dismissed as stress due to the mission.

They reported her as being a sensual goddess who knew how to be a vixen for her husband at the right time he needed her. They reported her as being a forgiving saint that understood his need for companionship with losing her. The papers were even forgiving of Martin for having a relationship with Ava.

What the papers nor Ella knew were that Martin missed Ava's supple body ready for him at a moment's notice. He missed her pregnant belly, her smell, and the moments he could tie her up and play with her any way he desired.

24

A HERO RETURNED

Ella attended the gala welcoming her home with Martin at her side. The press wanted to interview her experience and what happened in her accident and in the colony. She was trying to figure out how she would address the things that happened in the colony without revealing the seven years that passed, the relationship that developed with her research partner, and the three children they had together. The three children Martin didn't know about and the press would annihilate her over if they knew.

She wore a red dress with waves of silver beads streaking across the length of her torso and down the side of her leg. Martin chose the dress for her in hopes that he could separate any of the images of Ava the press would use to compare the two women. Somewhere in the crowd, Ava watched from a distance wearing a dress that wrapped snugly around her pregnant body, hoping Martin would see her.

Martin saw her and chose not to acknowledge her presence. He knew if he did, the press would focus on his choice to speak with her instead of focusing on the strides in research and exploration Ella had made. Ella's press conference began and Ava sauntered into view.

"Colonel Jones, how did you get trapped on the planet for these last few months?" A reporter asked.

"I had an accident. An animal on the planet charged me while I was out collecting samples. I was injured and bleeding, knocked unconscious. Major Gordon had to decide quickly how to save my life. He decided that the closest medical care was at the permanent colony and that we were able to get to it with the remaining fuel and oxygen supply we had. He expected that supplies and assistance would be provided by Alpha Base Camp to get us back home as quick as possible," Ella answered.

"Is Major Gordon alive?" Another reporter asked.

"Yes. He is still on the planet," she answered.

"Why didn't he come back with you?" The reporter questioned.

"I was under intense medical care from a debilitating disease and came back to get medical help on Earth. I had every intention on returning and rescuing them — him," she answered, realizing she almost revealed the secret she was keeping locked away.

"When will you be returning to the planet for the rescue mission?" A reporter asked.

"Well, that's where it gets more complicated. There is a problem with the wormhole connecting to Alpha Base Camp. It collapsed and we are trying to determine if we can find it. We think it is due to a solar storm on the planet and I am tasked with studying the impacts of the storm and if we can get the wormhole connection back," she explained.

~

As the attention of the reporters were now fully on Ella, Martin navigated to the side of the hall that was closest to Ava's location. He asked one of the servers to give a message to Ava as he disappeared into a side room. He made sure all of the windows were closed and covered to prevent any photographs being taken, just in case a photographer was lurking in the shadows.

A few moments later, Ava entered the room. Martin's stomach flipped over when he saw her in the blue dress that wrapped around her pregnant body, hugging the beautiful curves that became more voluptuous and soft as her pregnancy progressed. He saw that she bolted the door to maintain their privacy. She smiled like a cat who just had some cream.

"Martin, it has been a few days," she said. "I can tell you missed me." He was aroused and tried to ignore the reaction his body had to her.

"Ava, you can't just come to events like this. It isn't appropriate," he stated. She laughed softly.

"So, I shouldn't support the mother of the babies I'm carrying?" She asked.

"Ava, I got you a suite at the nicest hotel in the city," he said.

"And it is very lonely. You didn't check up on me like you said you would," she purred.

"I was planning on stopping by to make sure you were okay," he explained.

"I have needs, Martin. Needs that are not being met," she said as she unbuttoned the slit of her dress that ran up her leg to be able to sit down. When she sat, the slit opened and trailed the inside of her thigh up to her hip. The lace of her panties, the panties she wore for him that aroused her as she walked, peeked out at the edge of the slit.

"Ava, what are you doing?" He asked.

"Am I still beautiful?" She asked him. He definitely thought she was beautiful as she stretched her arms out on the back of the couch and uncrossed her legs. Her breasts pushed at the edge of her gown, looking like they would leap out for him with a deep inhale from her. He could smell that she was wet and ready for him, and he loved the way Ava smelled.

Before he could think about the consequences of his actions, he walked toward her and reached between her legs and he kissed her.

"Listen to me carefully. Don't move your arms. Spread your legs. Don't make a sound," he ordered as she shook her head to agree to his demands.

He popped her breasts out from her dress and sucked on her nipples hard. Being just a few months from birth and having twins, she had some milk enter into his mouth. He moaned at the taste and became rigid and ready to burst. He lifted her hips to him, letting the dress fall behind her, and she wrapped her legs around him while supporting her torso with her arms on the back of the couch.

He entered her quickly and she gasped quietly, remembering how he filled her up completely and stretched her to capacity. He was slow with her in his movement, savoring the minute quivering he felt inside of her. He let her desire build with his rhythm, flicking the bud between the folds of her mound to excite her and lead her to an intense climax. Then he felt the muscles inside of her spasm around him and tighten. He picked up the speed and intensity of his thrusts in her until she needed to scream out but bit her bottom lip. He kissed her as he continued to thrust into her, and she moaned into his mouth as he muffled her noises of ecstasy. He came into her filling her with every part of him. He realized in that moment that he saw her as the mother of his children and that a sexual union with her felt religious to him. He needed her desperately.

"Ava, I will come to you during the week. I won't live without you again," he said. "Now go out the connecting door and clean yourself up in the ladies' room. We can't be seen together here if we are to see each other again. Are you able to keep us a secret?"

"Are you saying I will be your mistress?" She asked.

"I suppose I am. We'll work out the details and a contract this week. Can you be satisfied with being my mistress?" He asked.

"Right now, yes. But if she leaves again, I want you for good. I want you forever," Ava stated.

"Yes, if she leaves again," Martin agreed knowing that Ella was not going to leave again. He could now have the best of both women, and he felt powerful.

MARTIN WALKED BACK into the ballroom and met up with Ella. She looked at him strangely but dismissed it with all the press around them. Once they left she addressed her concerns.

"Martin, are you feeling okay? You were flushed back there," she stated.

"I think something didn't settle well on my stomach. I started to feel a little ill," he lied.

"Oh, that's too bad. I had a surprise for you when we got home," she teased.

"Just let me shower when we get home. I'm sure that will help me feel better," he stated. He needed to be squeaky clean for Ella, incase her surprise led to intimacy.

Once home, he went straight for the shower. When he emerged in a towel, Ella lay there in a leather corset that lifted and revealed her breasts, the illusion of panties that were elastic strings running down between her legs, and her holding a whip out to him. He immediately found the straps to buckle her wrists above her head and her ankles to the posts of the bed, turned her over on her belly, and bound her in place.

With every smack of the whip on her buttocks, his manhood hardened. He lubricated her to make her ready for him and thrust into her vigorously. While he was enjoying himself, he realized he was far from orgasming. So he decided to experiment with his wife.

He pulled her braid back as he straddled her bound hands. Then he thrust inside of her mouth, having her test herself on him. The idea caused him to become more aroused, since she would never have done that three months ago. Something changed her. This was a new Ella he was married to. While he was close, he still wasn't orgasming. So he maneuvered back around to behind her and began lubricating her backside. She tensed.

He made a shushing sound as he placed a ball gag in her mouth and strapped it behind her head. She was panicked at how she had given herself over to Martin. He rubbed her from the pearl of her mound, into her, and up to the opening of her buttocks. He was causing her to feel pleasure as he attended to every crevice between her legs. He brought out her vibrator and began rubbing it from pearl to opening and back, causing an orgasm to begin.

In the middle of the orgasm he entered her backside and slowly pushed himself into her. She felt a different sensation of pleasure as she orgasmed and spasmed from the vibrator filling her. He began thrusting slowly in rhythm with his movements of her vibrator, rubbing and filling her in her center and bum, causing an explosion of pleasure through her entire being. Then he orgasmed into her, throbbing into the changed woman who allowed him to love her completely.

Afterwards, they took a shower together. He gently washed her, knowing she would need special care after her first night of sexual intercourse in her bum. She gasped and flinched into him as he washed her, which aroused him again. Being completely washed, He took her in the shower, holding her body against the shower wall as he thrust into her body wrapped around his. She was now ruined for any other man to ever pleasure her again, even David if he ever returned to Earth with their children. Her husband had remade her to fit him perfectly.

25

VISITATION

Martin arrived at the hotel suite with a contract two days later. He meant to provide Ava with everything she needed and wanted. He knew he loved her in ways he could never feel for Ella. Ava was having his children, even if the eggs had been Ella's.

Ava answered the door in a dress that flowed around her belly. It was a simple dress that accentuated her full breasts but had a flowing skirt that swayed with her hips as she walked. Martin imagined what she wore under the dress, if anything.

The sat at her table and he handed her the contract. She knew that signing the contract would secure her financially for the future, but would prevent her laying claim to Martin in any way. She was giving control over to him to visit her when he pleased and to leave her alone if he tired of her. Yet, his contract dictated that he would care and provide for her financially until she decided she wanted to date another man. The contract dictated that she could not interact with any other man during their arrangement. If she did, her contract would be null and void and she would no longer be provided for.

She signed the contract.

Once signed, Martin reached for her and kissed her. He reached under her dress to discover that she was bare and slick between her legs. He turned her away from him, leaned her over the table where her contract with him lay, and penetrated her from behind. He spent the afternoon with her, making her orgasm and burying himself into her. She found that the only way they could find pleasure with each other was with him behind her or her riding him. Her belly had gotten in the way with having twins.

When Martin left after a few hours, he told her he would bring her a copy of the signed and notarized contract in a few days. She closed the door, then sat on her couch naked and raw from his pounding into her, and cried. She wondered what she had just done in order to keep a man who was dedicated to a wife who could have his babies.

In retaliation, she made an appointment with a stylist the next day. By the time she walked out of the salon, her hair was in a dark brown bob with no trace of the copper hair he insisted she have. She took the credit card he'd given her and went to the closest lingerie store, buying the most expensive and alluring items to accentuate the parts of her body that he bought with his contract and the little piece of plastic in her hand.

PART 3

THE DISCUSSION

26

CHECK UPS

Ella went to her doctor for the mandatory check on her body to be sure the disease had not progressed. She waited quietly in the exam room hoping that if it had progressed there would at least be treatment options. The door opened with his nurse and items that an OB/GYN would use to take a Pap smear.

"So, Doc, what's that stuff for?" She asked jokingly.

"I need to check something, Ella," he said. "Lay back and put your feet in these stirrups."

Her doctor here had never examined her in this way, so she was concerned and uneasy. He made a 'hmph' noise that made her even more uneasy.

"Can you bring the ultrasound machine in here?" He asked the nurse. She left as he covered Ella up and kept the exam room door open. She rolled back into the room with the machine and turned the lights off. He squeezed the gel on her exposed stomach and pressed the wand into her abdomen, rubbing it back and forth. He didn't seem completely satisfied, so he got the internal ultrasound wand out, placed a condom over it, and gelled it.

He then inserted it into her and started moving it around.

He nodded to the nurse and she turned the monitor toward Ella and turned on the volume. A steady heartbeat fluttered on the monitor with the beating sound Ella heard. The doctor started taking measurements of the life inside of her. Then as he moved the wand around taking measurements.

"So, I would say you are pregnant, Colonel Jones. Congratulations!" The doctor told her. The nurse left the room with the machine. The doctor closed the door.

"I'm what?" She said.

"About three months along," he said.

"That's impossible. Martin and I have only been intimate for two of the three months I have been back. I was in a coma for a month," she stated.

"The measurements say three months. Did you have unprotected sex with anyone else before you saw Martin?" He asked.

"Like when I was in a coma? Not that I am aware of," she said.

"It also looks like, from what I could feel in the exam that this is not your first child," he stated staring directly at her, waiting on what she would say next.

"You knew I couldn't have children before, so why would you say that to me?" She asked, hoping it would shame him into remaining quiet about his exam.

"Well, you have had at least one other pregnancy, if not more," he said. She sighed and looked down. This doctor would not be shamed in to silence by her.

"I did have two pregnancies on the planet. Time was different there," Ella stated. "Seven years passed and we had no contact with Earth. The base camp cut us off and refused to provide us with help."

"Seven years is a long time to be celibate. So, who was he?" The doctor asked.

"David. We married while there and had three children. Please don't tell Martin. He wouldn't be able to understand," she begged.

"This is David's child, isn't it?" The doctor asked. Ella thought about it, wondering how she could have conceived when they had just had two babies a couple months prior. Then she remembered the night before she left. He had been so concerned that it would be her last night before the procedure, that he had attended to her every need and made sure she would remember him as she healed over the course of months in the hospital. Then the wormhole happened and it must have pushed his seed up into her further, resulting in a third pregnancy with him.

"Oh, God, how am I going to deal with Martin? This will destroy him. We already have a surrogate having our babies because I couldn't have them," Ella fretted.

"For all I know, this is a medical miracle and Martin got you pregnant when you were together in the hospital that first night. It is close enough that an early birth of a healthy baby is not unusual," the doctor explained. He smiled at her and fudged the medical papers to state he measured wrong and she was actually two months pregnant. The nurse looked at him strangely and then at Ella when she saw the medical documentation had been revised.

ELLA CAME HOME to an empty house. Martin was out again making sure Ava was cared for as she carried their twins. Ella began looking through the baby store catalog and decided she would go out and order baby furniture. While there, she hired a designer to come into their home and redecorate the guest bedrooms into children's rooms.

Ella decided that the theme of the twins' room would be French Toile with white wood and molding on the bottom half of the wall. Her baby's room would be different. He or she would have a room the color of the lush valley that her home with David overlooked on the alien planet. It would be filled with lush materials in deep greens with orange to blue gradient on the upper wall. Her baby would see the colors its dad would see every day. She hoped one day he could meet their fourth child together. A child made in love — David's pure love for her.

She came back home to find the house still empty and still. She checked her phone and didn't see any calls or messages from Martin. It was 5:30pm now and he had normally left for work. She called his lab to see if he was working late. His secretary told her he had taken he afternoon off. So, Ella decided to go upstairs to take a nap.

Martin rushed home, knowing he had lost track of time with Ava. It was 7:30pm and he was supposed to have been home by 5:30pm. Ella had been to the doctor that day for a check, so he knew she would want to talk with him about the results. He had stopped to get her a gift to cover his mistake, which caused him to be even later than expected.

He got him at 7:45pm and snuck into the house. It was very quiet. He noticed that dinner had not been made, so he quickly ordered Chinese for them. He then crept upstairs and saw that Ella was asleep in their bed. He had taken a shower at Ava's suite, so he knew that Ella wouldn't suspect his involvement with Ava.

He had successfully met with Ava three afternoons this

week and determined that he would take long lunches twice a week, eat and work through lunch the rest of the week to make up for lost time, and shift his schedule on Fridays to come in three hours early to have a long afternoon with Ava at the end of the week. He made sure his work schedule was not impacted by his meetings with Ava. In fact, Ella's habit of going into her lab by 5:00am every morning gave him the chance to go in early to assure he had the freedom to take longer lunches to meet Ava's needs fully.

The one thing Martin made sure to do was take a shower at her suite before he left. She made him late by joining him and pleasuring him in the shower today. He shouldn't think of his time with Ava while his wife lay in front of him. He kissed her forehead and told her he was home.

"Mmm. Martin, why are you so late? Your lab told me you took the afternoon off," she said. *Damn the lab. He needed to tell them something different.*

"No, I had to leave early from that location to look at samples at another site. They must have misunderstood me. I'm sorry I was so late. I have something to make it up to you. Actually, I've been meaning to get this for you since you are about to be a first-time mother. I wanted to honor you," he lied as he held up a ruby pendant the color of raspberries surrounded in diamonds.

Ella sat up and pondered the gift sparkling in front of her. She smiled sweetly as Martin clasped it around her neck. Then he kissed her neck gently and cupped her breast with his hand.

"Martin, I need to tell you something before you figure it out from my purchases from the baby store," Ella said.

"Oh, you went shopping for the babies. That is so

sweet and motherly," he said feeling shameful for how late he stayed with Ava.

"I'm pregnant, Martin," Ella announced.

"What?" He questioned.

"We are pregnant. Two months pregnant. You got me pregnant that first night you woke me from a coma and showed me how much you missed me and needed to be with me, " she lied. He looked at her strangely. Then he looked at her belly. He touched her belly softly. Caressed it gently.

"I think we need to be very careful with this baby. We can't take any risks after everything we have been through to get pregnant. What if I'm too rough and hurt you or the baby? I'll make sure you have pleasure, but I just can't risk hurting you and the baby," Martin stated, looking at Ella like she was a fragile piece of glass. The same way David looked at Ella before she left the planet. The way that made Ella feel broken and useless.

27

AVA

Martin continued to visit Ava three times a week. She began to tire with having twins. One of the visits she discussed how the three of them needed to go to an OB/Gyn visit together. Martin told her that it was within her right to not have Ella at the visits, that it was written in her surrogacy contract.

What was in the contract for the Natural Conception and Pregnancy contract for surrogates, was that the fathers of the babies could be a part of the OB/Gyn visits. It was part of the Natural process. Yet, the mothers who provided the eggs caused the inappropriate hormones to release to the baby, because it made the surrogate feel like she was going to lose the babies she carried. So the process was to be treated like an adoption scenario instead of a traditional surrogate scenario.

Ava was pleased with this arrangement, since it would mean she would have Martin to herself without Ava around. She would be able to pretend that he was her husband as he touched her stomach filled with his babies.

They went to the appointment and saw the two babies.

The doctor measured them to see that one baby was measuring smaller than the other one. So, the doctor scheduled an amniocentesis two days away to be sure the babies were fine. Ava was completely alarmed. Martin took her to her suite and called Ella to let her know he was staying to console Ava since the she received alarming news. She understood and offered to come over to help, but Martin told her he would be home by 5:00pm and she should take the time to rest. Ella was tired, so she agreed to let him handle this.

Martin led Ava to the bed and unwrapped her dress. He noticed that she had changed out of the demure undergarments she'd worn to the appointment. What he found was sheer fabric that was so alluring to him, he ripped the material off of her. He maneuvered her hips to the edge of the bed and stood over her, teasing her wetness with the tip of his cock. She squirmed and moaned to have him inside of her, but he resisted. He rubbed the tip along her full length, catching at her bud, circling it. He got a vibrator out and rubbed it along her sex until she was panting in desire, almost to her climax. Then he buried himself in her, keeping the vibrator against her, moving it in time with his thrusts. She reached the pinnacle of her desire, screamed out his name, and spasmed around his member. He thrust faster, ready to orgasm with her. They moved in time, knowing each other's rhythm and timing. As he orgasmed she spasmed around him.

Like always, he took a shower, kissed her sweetly, and left to go home to his wife.

~

MARTIN CAME to take her to her doctor's appointment again. He held her hand the whole time the amniocentesis was being done. The doctors left the room with the emergency genetic tests to determine if everything was fine with the babies. What they found was unexpected.

The twins were half siblings. Apparently, the timing of the implantation and hormones to induce implantation coincided with Ava ovulating. She conceived a child with Martin during the Natural Conception night. What the doctors that night had not realized was that Martin decided to not use a condom. In fact, most men didn't actually have sex with the surrogate mothers, but enacted a scenario that played out that they were having sex while still fully clothed. Martin took the scenario too far. Now Ava was having a baby they conceived together, which made things complicated.

When Ava and Martin were told this, both were thrilled. Ava was thrilled since she would have the right to keep one of the babies, which meant she got to share Martin with Ella forever. Martin was thrilled since this meant he had naturally conceived with both Ava and Ella. He had yet to tell Ava the Ella was pregnant. The best part was that the second baby was slightly smaller because of the delayed development. Both babies were healthy.

Martin took her back to her suite and fucked her long and hard. He took his shower, kissed her, and left to go home to Ella.

FRIDAY ARRIVED and Martin came to her at 2:00pm. She was eight months pregnant and beginning to feel a bit ill. Martin suggested he run her a bath. He got in the tub with her and sat behind her. As she leaned back on him, he reached around and massaged her, circling her sensitive bud with his finger, rubbing down and into her center, bringing her to slow desire. Due to the size of her stomach. She couldn't face him, but he knew that the water in the tub helped her feel less heavy.

He nudged her onto her knees and angled his shaft at her center. She pushed back taking his full length into her and slowly rocked in rhythm with his thrusting. They orgasmed together and he remained nestled inside of her as she leaned back in the tub against him.

"I love you, Ava," he whispered in her ear as he nuzzled her neck. He'd never said that to her before.

"I love you, too," she told him back.

He helped her from the tub and took her to the bed. He curled up naked behind her, savoring the sweet moments with the woman having his children. Nestled with the woman who never had trouble conceiving his child, who sucked his seed into her and defied the odds of conception. This woman he needed desperately to be with her every aching moment he could. She wasn't fragile. She was strong and he felt at ease loving her naturally and at his whim.

He hugged her placing his hands on her stomach. Drifting up the fondle her breasts.

"Martin, please stay the night. I want you through the night. I need you inside of me tonight," Ava pleaded.

"Okay, I'll stay." He texted Ella that Ava had called him with contractions. He told her he thought he should stay with her and sleep on her couch in case they got closer. He would call her if they went to the hospital. Ella texted back to tell Ava good luck and best wishes.

He silenced his phone and proceeded to make love to Ava off and on through the night. That morning she went into full labor and they headed into the hospital.

28

BIRTH

Ava was dilated and effaced enough that the doctors told her she was too far along to have an epidural. These doctors were unaware that Ava and Martin were not married. The congratulated Martin on getting Ava through the first part of labor with love making and orgasms. He was grateful Ella was not there to hear that comment.

Labor was a sensual experience for Ava. With every contraction she asked Martin to manipulate her sex until she orgasmed. She orgasmed every time. He was so aroused at one point that she offered to give him oral pleasure to get him off. He happily obliged since the doctors insisted that they needed to refrain from intercourse while she was this far into labor.

He didn't call Ella for the birth. Ava requested that she have this special time with Martin, especially since one of the babies was theirs. Martin agreed. After a full day in labor, Ava gave birth to the first baby. Five minutes later she had the second baby. The first baby to be born was the one she conceived with Martin. He was healthy and had a lusty cry.

The second baby was still. The child was sent to the Neonatal Intensive Care Unit. The child was struggling. She had a defective heart that couldn't pump the blood needed to circulate her blood. They had to put her on a machine to pump her blood for her. The doctor examined her fully and advised that he and his wife say their goodbyes to their daughter. He called Ella to rush to the hospital. Within an hour the baby that shared Martin and Ella's blood died in her arms. Ella was horrified. But then she asked about the other baby.

Martin sat with Ella and explained the situation. He explained that she had conceived at some point after the implantation due to the hormones she had to take. Ella crumbled inside knowing that was exactly how she had conceived her first child with David. Those hormones that accepted his seed over Martin's. Those hormones that allowed Ava to give the one thing to Martine that she never could. Ella left the hospital alone that night, because she knew Martin wanted to be with his child, the child that would never come home to Ella.

MARTIN AND AVA kept up the cycle of their affair. He could now make excuses to stay longer, or visit after work, because he wanted to spend time with his son. Ava had read that if she breast fed she would have natural pregnancy prevention. Martin loved the idea of still having sex with her without a condom impeding their lovemaking. He also knew that she couldn't take birth control of any sort while breast feeding. He wanted the best for his son.

Yet, Ava was very fertile. She conceived another baby

after six months, the same night Ella went into labor. Martin missed the text from Ella that her water had broken. He was in the middle of burying himself in Ava as her body sucked his seed straight to the ovulated egg awaiting to be penetrated with life. There was something special between the intercourse that night with Ava and Martin. The both felt the world shift and knew something had happened between them.

Then he checked his phone to see that Ella was at the hospital. He rushed off forgetting to take his ritual shower.

Ella was in pain. She needed an epidural. She didn't handle the stress of birth well. Martin tried to touch her, but she shooed him away from her. He tried to console him, but she told him to stop. She needed complete silence from him.

When the baby was born, his skin was very fair and his hair was red. Martin had olive skin, so he assumed the baby took after Ella with her red hair. Ella saw her son and realized he looked exactly like his sisters and brother did when they were born. Martin suggested they name him after David, since he had saved Ella's life. She agreed and secretly knew he was named after his father. The baby was David Gordon Jones.

29

DISCOVERY

Martin spent the first few weeks attentive to Ella and their new family. Little David proved to be a handful and nocturnal, keeping them up through the night. So after a few weeks, Martin made excuses that he needed to get sleep for work and proceeded to go back to his affair with Ava and staying later each night at work to make up for the long lunches he would take to spend the middle of the day with Ava.

Martin's first Friday afternoon with Ava involved him attending a lamaze class with her to prepare for the birth of their child, a child Ella was unaware of. After the class Martin drove her back to her apartment and they walked in holding hands. He looked at her, the way her face glowed in pregnancy and how her slight frame carried their baby gracefully. She was alluring to him.

She walked ahead of him into the apartment to light a few candles. Her hips swayed gracefully under her dress, calling to him to hug and embrace her. As she turned towards him, he admired the full bosom she had developed in pregnancy. He longed to see her soft body naked in front of him in the candlelight. In that moment, Martin realized he had truly fallen in love with Ava and would do anything she asked of him.

She looked up at him through her lashes and smiled warmly. He walked toward her and wrapped his arms around her, leaning down to kiss her. He murmured his love for her and she started to disrobe. He stopped her and just held her and shook his head that was not what he was expecting. Then he put his hands on her cheeks and looked directly into her her eyes.

"Ava, I love you. I love you with all my heart and will never leave you," he stated directly. A tear fell down her cheek after waiting to finally hear those words from Martin.

"Martin, I need you, every part of you now," Ava stated unbuckling his belt seductively.

"I guess I can't deny the needs of the woman carrying my baby," he said with a chuckle.

Afterwards, they lay naked under a blanket on her couch nestling each other closely. She lay along her side on him with her head on his chest dozing off and on. The light was falling into dusk outside and he failed to notice as he snuggled with Ava devoured by her soft skin and steady breathing as she slept. He felt at peace with her.

Ella noticed that Martin had not come home yet that evening. Little David was sleeping soundly and she had taken the chance to make a romantic meal for Martin upon coming home from work. The candles on the table stood dormant and unlit with the box of matches on the table waiting to be struck. She placed the meal she had made in the oven to stay warm, but grabbed a plate for herself since she needed to have nourishment for breast-feeding.

She was alone and felt like her role as a mother to her son and wife to Martin was such a different experience than what she had experienced with David. David, the man who built a home overlooking the valley for her, to help her feel like she had a home with him. Now she wondered why she had ever left, but remembered that she had become a burden to him, incapable of caring for herself in her physical disability. The disability that no longer existed.

She was truly dissatisfied with this evening and how Martin had not come home at his normal time. So, she decided to be productive and go through their storage room to organize it into her new office while she stayed at home with Little David. As she dug through the random boxes Martin had stored she noticed that there was a box labeled strangely.

She was used to their files being labeled as secure or top secret to make sure neither would look into government files or projects they did not have access to. But this box was labeled as "Not for Ella." So, like a kid who hates to be told no, Ella took the blade and untaped the edges of the file box and laid the lid to the side.

The first thing Ella saw was the memorial images from her and David's ceremony. She sighed deeply on seeing the image of David on the page in front of her. She caressed his image with her finger gently, making sure she didn't rub him away. She lifted the glossy magazine and turned to the article on the memorial ceremony. It was difficult to read and know that Martin had to experience losing her as his wife and mourn her.

The next magazine was a tabloid that focused on Martin standing with a woman at the memorial. What she noticed was how he looked at the woman. She recognized that look. He had looked at her in that way when she returned home from the alien planet. Then she lifted the magazine to see the image closer and she recognized the woman. It was Ava, David's fiancé.

Ella began flipping through the pages of the tabloid to see the revealing images of Martin and Ava in the master bedroom of their house. The worst image was Martin pressing Ava's back against the full length window that looked out to the ocean, with her wrapped around his body as they were clearing having sex. The images were taken on the night of her and David's memorial service. Tears began falling down her cheeks.

She continued to pull out the magazines from the box to see tabloid images of their three-month escapade and affair. Magazines reported on their affair and gushed over their support of each other in such difficult times. Then the stories turned into the questions of whether they were to be a serious couple and if they were finding a new love match with each other. Their affair was romanticized. Yet, Ella saw that in the images Martin always looked at Ava with a soft desire that truly ran deep. He looked at her in a way that he never looked at her. He was always just slightly distant from her, in his own world.

So, Ella decided that she would display all the contents of the box on their coffee table and with on Martin to come home. She fell asleep on the couch waiting on his arrival.

30

COMING HOME

Martin entered the quiet house at 10:00pm. He had lost track of time at Ava's. In fact, he had resisted leaving the warm nest she created for them. He felt sheltered from reality when with her. Now he was walking back into reality, and he tensed at the moment he would face Ella as he entered their home at such a late hour.

He tried to think of what he could say to her to explain why he was so late. He knew that he would need to show her affection to appease his absence, the affection that he knew no longer came from a place of love. At some point his heart and desire had made a 160 degree turn. He now loved Ava and felt only lust for the woman who was his wife. He felt exhausted at the thought he would need to show her affection and perform.

Then he saw her sleeping soundly on the couch. She looked peaceful and he couldn't remember when he last saw her sleeping for any length of time. The baby had deprived her of sleep. The baby he couldn't bond with, that annoyed him and was destroying his marriage. Yet, he knew he was just as much at fault for the destruction of his marriage. He couldn't blame it all on the child.

He walked towards Ella on the couch to cover her up with the blanket. As he approached her, he saw the tabloids and magazines he had stored and sealed, spread out on their coffee table. The images she had them turned to brought back memories of nights he'd had with Ava early on. The memories aroused him and he shut his eyes in shame.

He decided that the only thing he could do was dote on his wife and attempt to distract her momentarily. So he leaned over her and whispered to her that he missed her, and that they should take advantage of the baby sleeping. In her half awake state she mumbled something to him that turned into a moan as he touched her deftly between her legs, after weeks of not being touched. Before she was fully awake, he lifted her hips and plunged himself into her, rocking her into arousal that she desperately needed. She wrapped her legs instinctively around him and clung to him as they rocked in time with each other. Then her release came and she started to moan, but he covered her cry with his mouth to prevent from waking the baby.

He kept pushing himself into her, not finishing like he normally did. Martin held her hips pulling them to him as he surged forward, plunging himself deeply into her. Then he pulled out and turned her over. He pushed himself into her from behind, holding onto her hips, positioning himself further into her. She started to release again and he put his fingers in her mouth to prevent her from crying out. He knew he was holding back from climaxing, making sure she was completely pleasured before he did. When she was shaking under him, he released into her. He left her curled up on the couch and went to take a shower.

The next morning he woke to his wife sitting in front

of the magazines and tabloids in front of her at the dining table, looking at him over the rim of her coffee mug, expecting an answer. He just stared at her quietly. He went to get a cup of coffee and sat down across from her. Then he spoke.

"I thought you were dead. They told me you were dead," he stated.

"You didn't take long to have an affair with Ava," Ella stated plainly as she pointed to the first night of photos that were taken.

"We were sad and lonely. You had been gone for over three months without communication. I was also angry at you for deciding to go on an expedition when you were scheduled to transmit home." Martin was explaining himself, possibly over explaining, so he quieted down.

"Ah, mad at me for not transmitting. So, on the day of my funeral is when you started an affair with Ava. Couldn't you two at least wait a week or a few days?"

"I can see how that could be seen. I'm sorry for that. But she was really sad and I was really lonely. We were two consenting adults and there was nothing that bound us from comforting each other." Martin was firm in his position.

"I understand that. I shouldn't be so hard on you, especially since…" she began as a tear rolled down her cheek as she thought of her children and David whom she left behind.

Something inside Martin shriveled, since he was expecting a fight with her. Instead, she backed off and began to change the direction of the conversation.

"Especially since what?" He asked since she had paused and not resumed what she had started to say.

"David and I were stranded. We felt so alone and distraught over the mission refusing to rescue us. There was a transmission that we made from the permanent colony, and attempt we made to get them to rescue us. They refused and cut the transmission and the ability to contact them in the future off."

"Ella, you never told me that. That is horrible. But you got back to the base camp in three months, so not so long."

"Time doesn't work like that on the planet when you are away from the Base Camp. We were stranded for seven years."

Martin just looked at her in disbelief. He was trying to process how she still looked as young as she did when seven years had passed for her. It would make her almost ten years older, but she shoed no signs of aging.

"Another thing that I didn't tell you was that I was mortally wounded during a research expedition with David. He saved my life and nursed me to health in the permanent colony for at least three months. I owed him my life. That creates a bond between people."

"I can understand how trauma creates a bond between people. Your deaths were a trauma for Ava and me," Martin looked directly at Ella to determine if she truly understood him.

"David and I thought you and Ava were lost to us forever. Actually, David and Ava were not even engaged anymore. They had broken up in the last visit home," Ella informed him. Martin was a little stunned by this since Ava had still been serving in the role of fiancé at the memorial service. It explained why David's family refused to interact with her.

"One thing led to another, and we developed deep feelings for each other," she told him, leaving out the part where she and David had developed romantic feelings for each other during the first mission period, feelings that had led to sexual encounters they had while out on expeditions.

"You were stranded together, so I can see how that would happen," Martin stated, hoping that this was the conversation where they told each other everything.

"We married each other. We had two children together, daughters. He was so kind and loving. But I left them because my disease progressed and I needed medical help. I intended to tell you everything and keep things neat between us. But when you helped me come out of my coma and made love to me with such passion, I got all confused. I intended to return to them, but I got pregnant. We got pregnant."

"We have a beautiful boy together. He looks so much like you."

"Martin, I love you but I have so many conflicting emotions. I miss my girls. I miss David. Yet, I don't want to give you up or leave my son. This is an impossible situation, and I'm so sorry. I have no room to judge you when I am dealing with this."

"Well, let's get everything out on the table then. I was about to propose marriage to Ava when you came back." Ella just stared at Martin in disbelief, but kept her mouth shut. "She got pregnant."

"Just like that? After all the time it took for us to try?" Ella asked.

"Yeah. Doesn't seem fair, does it?" He said. "I have been going to see her during her pregnancy, to make sure she is cared for."

"What? What type of going to see her?" Ella asked.

"It started off with innocent and honorable intentions. Ella, she is as irresistible as you are. I can't say no to either of you. I also have decided that I will continue to care for her and the child."

"I get and understand financial support and visiting the

baby, but the 'you can't say no to her' part is upsetting. How long have you been doing this?"

"A while now."

"During my pregnancy? The late nights that you left me here on my own? Were you with her when I went into labor? Is that where you were?" Ella was crying as she asked these questions.

"Yes."

"Were you with her last night?"

"Yes. I'm sorry that I lost track of time."

"Martin, either we end or you and Ava end."

"But you want to go back to David!" He spat back at her. She froze at his words, knowing that they were the truth, but a truth she was denied. She sat down on the couch in defeat. She had no way to solve their problems, no way to keep her new family in tact when Ava held sway. She put her face in her hands.

"Let me see if we can try things to find a solution that works for everyone," Martin suggested.

"What does that mean?" Ella asked.

"Doing things nontraditionally."

31

COMPROMISES

Ava had her baby girl two weeks later. Martin would visit her but had to refrain from any sexual interactions, as is normal after having a baby. For three months Ava focused on her new baby girl, Alexandra, and seemed to not be attracted to Martin. He was confused by this and completely at a loss, since she was absolutely breathtaking to him as she nursed their child. He brushed this off as something normal that happened to women.

Yet, Ella was not like this after having their baby boy. She counted down the days until they could have sex again. So, Martin was surprised when Ava was not like Ella. He ended up spending more time at home with Ella and their child, since Ava wouldn't let Martin help even change a diaper when he was there, and he wasn't capable of breastfeeding. She made sure she was in complete control of the situation.

The time Martin spent with Ella was at first strained. But after time elapsed, they relaxed and settled into a schedule that suited them both. Martin decided to begin helping Ella research ways to get the mission opened so they could make contact with David and her daughters. The goal was to bring them home. So far, Martin was reaching dead ends with getting his financial backers to agree to a meeting to discuss the issue.

Ella was up against similar problems. Every meeting she had to insist that David needed to have a chance to come home was met with safety issues. Either it was too dangerous to bring him back through the wormhole, since they decided the wormhole was unstable, or refunding the mission was too expensive. Ella was beginning to feel that bringing David and her daughters home to Earth was hopeless.

When she walked in that evening after being told that the mission wouldn't be funded again, Martin recognized her sadness. He went over and pulled her coat off of her and wrapped her in his arms in a warm embrace. She broke down and cried into his chest.

"They said no again?" He asked, already knowing that was the case. He knew her too well.

"Yeah. Wormhole is too unstable, so they won't fund a rescue mission that could kill people," she answered.

"You are stressed out and tense. How about I give you a massage?" Martin suggested.

"That would be nice," she stated with a warm smile.

"I also have a surprise for you, something new we can try," he stated.

"New?" She asked him with a sly look.

"Yeah, spice things up a little. If you are okay with it, I would like to try something new with you," he stated.

"Martin, right now, I am up for anything to take my mind off of always being told no." She sighed and collapsed on the couch before they ate dinner.

32

BONDING

Martin strapped Ella with leather cuffs to their bed. He had placed a rubber sheet on the mattress and taken all their bedding off. It was neatly folded and stored in their closet out of sight. Candles were lit in the room and he had hypnotic music playing in the background. Ella had always refused to agree to letting him tie her up, but what she saw was sensual and romantic.

The first thing he did was shave her hair off until she was completely bald between her legs. He wanted her smooth. He wanted to see every part of her, to know the moment she was slick for him. The foam he used had a warming cinnamon sensation that would both taste good and arouse her more. As he shaved her slowly, she moaned and occasionally gasped as he moved her sensitive skin around for the shaving process.

Once complete, he poured warm water over her slowly, making sure to pour the stream of water over her most sensitive areas and wiped her down with his hands to clean all traces of hair away. With the motions of his fingers in his cleaning, he massaged her, flicking his fingers in and out of her, to arouse and excite her. Though she was ready, he refrained and dried her off and the sheet beneath her.

His next stage was to blindfold her. He didn't want her to see what he was going to do. He knew that to know what was going to happen diminished the impact of arousal. So to deny Ella of sight would give her increased arousal and desire once he began touching her again. He proceeded and Ella responded. What he failed to ask her for was a word to let him know she had reached her limit. He didn't intend to expose her to pain, but his plan was to build her up to it in small increments until she was acclimated to his personal fantasy.

While she was blindfolded he took a knife and traced the point lightly across her breasts and down her stomach, so light that it registered as a tickle. She smiled feeling the sensation and flinch at one point, almost knocking her skin. In that moment she gasped in surprise. Martin retire the blade in that moment and then reached for his riding whip. He followed the same path with it, lightly tapping her nipples and stomach as he moved it along her body. When he reached her mound, he tap her quickly and lightly, enough to arouse her and cause her too whimper in need.

With each sound she made, he popped her with the whip. Each pop became harder as the blood rushed to her core and her body responded to the quick strikes that intensified. She writhed for a release, rocking her mound into the pop of the whip, hoping for that final peak. Martin stopped the strikes, aware that she was going to release before he was finished with her.

He put the whip away and then reached for a small vibrator. He traced it around her nipples and down the center of her stomach leading to the delicate ease of her cleft. He dipped it between her folds edging toward her jewel. As he started this motion, he pressed the tip of his phallus into her center, giving her the pressure without the relief of being impaled and filled.

As he led her to increased desire and arousal, she pulled on the bindings, trying to meet his pressure to provide herself with relief. Her attempts were futile because he had her well constrained and controlled.

"Do you like this?" He asked as he pressed himself almost into her.

"Yes, please, Martin, please!" He chuckled knowing he was in complete control of her. He leaned down and nipped at her nipples, sucking hard and getting the test of milk, which almost led him to losing control. Instead he pulled away and unhooked her ankles. He flipped her over, causing her arms to cross and pushing her breasts out and up. He rebound her ankles, assuring her legs would remain spread no matter what he did. In that moment, he placed the tip of his phallus at her core and grabbed her hips to force her to remain still.

He strapped a harness around her hips and wedged the small vibrator at her jewel, causing her to groan with the constant vibration against her most sensitive spot. Then he pushed himself into her slowly, making sure she felt his full length that she began spasming around. As she reached her first peak, he moved to meet her spasms, pounding into her with force and pushing himself deeper into her. He wanted to fill her with his seed, fill her womb to bind her to him further.

The thought of her being filled with his seed made him lose control. He grabbed her hair and pulled her hair back. She cried out in pain as he continued to thrust into her. He grabbed her breast with his free hand and pinched her nipple, which caused her pain and him pleasure as he heard her cry out. Then he released into her, unhooking her wrists and laying onto of her, remaining inside of her as he pinned her to the bed.

"Mmm, that was so good," he said and bit her neck like an animal marking his mate. She lay under him, not sure of what just happened. She breathed shallowly. Her body was confused by the pleasure she felt from the pain he inflicted on her. Her body responded to his inflicted pain, while her mind revolted against what he was doing to her. Yet, she began to rationalize it away as something she just needed to get used to. If she didn't, she would lose him to Ava, the woman she knew was manipulative from what David had told her about his experiences with her.

Ella knew sex with Martin would never be the same, now that he knew her body responded to pain.

33

BREAKING POINT

Ella made a discovery in her research that showed a trace of residual energy from the wormhole they used in the mission. As she continued her research, she set up a monitor to track the spikes and surges in the energy traces she found. She did not share the information with Martin, but had no valid reason for her decision to keep it secret from him. He had been helpful, but something instinctually led her to not completely trust Martin and his intentions.

He had spent more time with her in the last six months, so she suspected that his visits to see Ava and the baby were minimal amounts of time. This also caused her to feel conflicted emotions, since the wanted Martin to spend time with his child but not spend time with Ava. She knew she was jealous of Ava and did not trust the woman's intentions and motivations. Yet, she was unsure of her own motivations for trying to bring David and her children home to Earth.

How would she navigate the issue of being legally married to Martin but emotionally bonded in personal vows to David? She knew why she wanted her children home, but David was her own conflict. She did not know how she felt about him without him with her in the present moment.

She did know how she felt about Martin. She knew that she was physically attracted to Martin, but her emotional bond with him was unraveling with his fathering a child with Ava. Additionally, her baby boy looked nothing like Martin and she suspected that he had not actually fathered her child. Little David could possibly be the son she wanted to give to the man she called husband in the permanent colony, the father of her daughters.

She sent her current research findings to a contact from the original mission she and David had started five years ago. She made sure the files were encrypted so Martin would not have access. She suspected that Martin had not been as supportive in finding assistance and financial backing for reopening the mission, but couldn't prove her suspicions. She had a gut feeling about this and was unsure of how to validate how she felt. So, she played her part as dutiful wife, grateful for his support, to prevent him from suspecting she was on to him.

Martin was attempting to plan an inventive night with Ella. His dream was to have a menagerie a trois, like many men fantasized about. He knew that this could be asking a lot of her, but he felt he had made progress with Ella and that she would be open to his suggestion. Now what he needed to make his fantasy a reality was to make the suggestion to Ava. He didn't want just any woman to join them, but to have the other woman he loved and had a child with would be perfect.

He slowly turned the key in the door, so as not to wake the baby, and entered into the lavish apartment he provided Ava. She knew he was coming over, so she wouldn't be surprised when he walked in. He didn't see her in the living room, so suspected she was in the nursery taking care of Alexandra. He went to the kitchen and decided to be sweet and make Ava lunch. He got out some eggs and began boiling them, knowing that she adored a Cobb salad.

"I smell bacon," Ava said as she entered the kitchen wearing a sheer pink gown that flared out at the top of her hips. The matching thong revealed that she had shaved herself smooth for him. Additionally, he saw something glint inside the thong, which she took notice of and smiled mischievously at him.

"Hmm, what's that?" He asked.

"Something you need to investigate closer," she said as she grabbed a piece of bacon, tracing her hand along his butt as she leaned past him. He turned the stove off, allowing the boiled eggs to settle for peeling later.

"Are you hungry?" He asked.

"For something other than food," she said. He leaned towards her, gently fondling her mound, finding her wet and ready. He removed his hand and sucked on his fingers that were slick from touching her. Then he lifted her onto the counter and pulled a chair up to devour her.

She tasted amazing, like cinnamon and spices mixed in honey. The little thing that glinted under the sheer fabric was a piercing that heightened her arousal. He fingered the jewel and she gasped as it rubbed against her clitoris. Martin smiled and licked her, flicking the new piercing deftly with his tongue. Ava buried her fingers in his hair and let out a moan. As he manipulated her with his tongue, he unbelted his pants and pushed them down, ready for her at any moment.

When he buried his tongue in her to taste her fully, she exploded. He pulled her off the counter and int his lap, her spasms enveloping his phallus. Then she began riding him, moving up and down his member to lengthen her orgasm. He wrapped his arms around her and carried her to the wall, bracing her back against it. Then he impaled her roughly and steadily, pushing his full length into her, letting gravity push her down around him.

The friction of his chest against her breasts made her leak out milk, which he sucked away hungrily. She cried out as he thrust into her and sucked at her breast simultaneously. She orgasmed again, clawing at his back, trying to pull him closer to her. Then he released, spilling himself into her. He carried her to the couch and lay her on top of him. He wanted to stay inside of her for as long as he could. She let him, hoping that this afternoon would never end.

"That was nice," he said quietly.

"Mmm, hmm," she answered.

"When did you get your little piercing?" He asked.

"A few weeks ago. It was why I wouldn't have sex," she stated.

"Oh! Well, it was a nice surprise," he said.

"I'm glad you like it."

"Well, since you are trying new things, would you be up for adding a little flavor into our trysts?"

"Flavor? Like what?"

"Well, would you be open to trying to add another woman to the mix?" He asked gingerly, not mentioning the other woman would be Ella.

"Who?" Ava asked with alarm.

"Well, Ella."

"Why?" Ava asked. Her happy mood was quickly diminishing.

"Well, I'm feeling torn between you two. I was thinking if you both could experience intimacy with me and each other, maybe some understanding could develop," Martin rationalized.

"So, you think that your wife and your mistress being intimate will solve you feeling torn between us? What are you expecting will be the outcome from this?" Ava asked.

"One of two things could happen. Either, you both become comfortable with each other, or I will end up having to choose between the two of you. It means that one of you will not spend time with me anymore," Martin stated without saying who the "one" would be. Ava felt uneasy, since she felt trapped as the woman who was receiving financial support from him based on providing him with his desires. So she folded.

"Okay, I'll try anything once."

Martin was elated and kissed Ava. He was so excited that he left without spending time with Alexandra.

Three weeks later, Martin invited Ava over. He'd gotten sitters for the babies and set the stage for Ella to experience something new. Ella was strapped down and blindfolded, awaiting the woman to enter the room. The music was playing in the background, preventing Ella from distinguishing who was in the room. All Ella knew was that she had agreed to allow Martin to have a menagerie a trois with another woman. She was very nervous.

Ava saw Ella and whispered to Martin if Ella was aware of who she was. He indicated that Ella wanted to be surprised, which made Ava uneasy. She started to insist that Ella be told, but Martin reminded her that he may need to make an immediate choice if she failed to commit to her agreement. Ava couldn't take away the lifestyle she and her daughter were living based on a single night, no matter how destructive it felt.

So, Ava took the feather and whip that Martin handed her as he sat in the chair in the corner watching their every move. She began dragging them softly down Ella's body. Ella responded with a small gasp and a smile. Ava ignored Martin's arousal as she focused her attention on Ella. She let her hair fall down on Ella's body and softly dragged her nails down her arms. She was trying to acclimate Ella to being touched by a woman. Ava was trying to acclimate herself to touching a woman.

Ava decided to nuzzle Ella's neck with kisses and nibbles, to show her it felt the similar. Ella moaned and furrowed her brows, indicating she was confused by her physical response. Ava knew that Ella was not yet relaxed and moved slowly. She kissed along Ella's jawline and then enveloped her mouth with a kiss. She prolonged the kiss until Ella's mouth relaxed and opened slightly, allowing Ava to dart her tongue in.

Ella had never been kissed by lips so soft and full. The nibbles along her neck were sharp but soft, and the lips pressed on hers felt nothing like the persistent and needy mouth that Martin had. This mouth moved slowly and when Ella opened her mouth in a sigh, the woman darted her tongue in, grazing Ella's tongue softly. Heat exploded in Ella's body. She felt like her lips were on fire, but she wanted more. Martin never made her feel in this way. She kissed the woman back, wishing she could wrap her arms around her and touch her.

Ava recognized that Ella was responding to her kisses. So, she ran her nails down her side and snuggled up next to Ella, prolonging her kisses. She draped her leg across Ella and intwined it with her leg. She gently rubbed her leg against Ella's which also grazed Ella's mound with the motion. Ella's arousal showed in the reaction of her nipples, which Ava circled softly with her nails before gently sucking and kissing them. Ella started to squirm, trying to press herself against Ava's leg and body.

So, Ava repositioned herself to straddle Ella, rubbing herself against her. Ella moaned and lifted her hips to meet Ava's. Ava reached down and touched Ella, manipulating her sex and feeling how slick she was. Ava was aroused that she had caused such a reaction in Ella. She unhooked one of Ella's hands and guided her hand to her sex. Ella touched Ava gently and shyly, but found the nerve that ran from her clitoris to her center. Ella surprised Ava with her deft manipulation, bringing her to a quick climax. Ella prolongs Ava's orgasm by plunging her fingers into her center and massaging her pulsing core.

Ava returned the favor and kissed Ella deeply. They smiled at each other, though Ella was still unaware of who the woman was. Before Ava could settle, Martin nudged her off of Ella and she watched as he plunged himself into her, thrusting over and over until he climaxed. He removed Ella's blindfold and unhooked her. The women made eye contact and Ella looked away.

Ava lay in the distance waiting to see what would happen next. She knew that if there were a choice to be made, he would not choose her. He had already chosen who he wanted.

34

FINDING DAVID

Ella listened intently to the sound waves and patterns that she had studied for the past few months. In the past three weeks she tracked a repeated pattern that occurred every twenty minutes. The steady pulse led Ella to believe that the wormhole was viable for reopening. She documented her findings and took them to the head of the original program for feedback. She also did not tell Martin about her findings.

The program director spoke privately with her on her research. He stated that the program would not fund a new mission, but that he could set up a covert system that would allow her to make the attempt to communicate with the permanent colony. The next few weeks revolved around setting up the operation in the location the program had shut down.

On the day she was to make her first transmission attempt, she made sure Martin had a dinner waiting for him at home. It was one of his late nights, those nights she knew he was with Ava. Something about the situation made her feel anxious and taken advantage of. She had lost all desire for Martin and while she had been physically attracted during her interaction with Ava, afterwards she felt completely disconnected emotionally and sexually in her marriage. Martin had taken things too far for her comfort, so if Ava could provide entertainment for him and give her time alone, she felt at peace with it.

Additionally, she brought Little David along with her. The baby was quiet and peaceful when he was with her. She always felt centered when around her baby boy — David's baby boy.

The instruments board lit up as she turned the switches, readying the system to begin transmitting to the planet. Her program director arrived around 6:00 pm with cups of coffee and a snack that would sustain them for the next few hours.

"You ready to try this?" He asked her in his upbeat way.

"Yeah," Ella responded flatly, trying not to get her hopes up.

He turned the knobs to the transmission setting and started the transmission to determine if he could get the correct signal for the transmission. In about five minutes they began receiving transmission pulses that indicated something was picking up on their signals. He repeated the standard transmission in a loop and recorded it, so they could send the looped message and wait until there was a response.

An hour passed by and Ella began dozing off as she held Little David after his feeding. Then a different sound transmitted through the system. Ella awoke from her semi-sleep when she heard the different transmission. The program coordinator started dialing the instruments to clear up and focus the transmission. Then they heard the voice on the other end.

"This is the permanent colony. Is anyone out there?" rang the woman's voice across the distance of space and time. Ella lay Little David down gently in his travel bassinet and approached the instruments. She sat down at the desk and reached out to press the receiver, her hand trembling as she reached forward.

"This is Ella Jones transmitting from Earth to permanent colony," she said into the microphone. There was silence.

"Ella Jones? Are you the Ella that went to Alpha Base Camp?" The voice questioned.

"Yes," Ella answered as she looked downward feeling shame.

"Mom?" The voice asked. Ella's inhaled sharply and a tear rolled down her cheek.

"Lilly?" Ella questioned.

"Mom! Why did you leave us?" She asked.

"My disability was getting worse and your dad wasn't going to benefit from caring for me. I needed medical help on Earth," Ella explained.

"But you didn't come home…" the woman sounded distraught.

"I couldn't come home. The wormhole collapsed," she answered.

"Mom, you've been gone so long," Lillian stated.

"How many years, baby?" Ella asked, pondering the worst.

"I'm twenty-two years old now. Dad' almost fifty now," she explained. Ella laid her head down and just started crying.

"Hi, Lillian, this is Commander Stanton. We are reopening the wormhole now that it is stable. Only thing is that we need everyone to come through the wormhole in one go. This is a rescue mission and the only time I am able to open it. Do you understand what I am saying?" He directed her.

"Yes. We've been waiting for supplies for so long. We need medicine. Will you sen that through first so we can stabilize some of my patients?" She asked seriously.

"Yes, I can send medical triage supplies in the travel pods we have remaining. The travel needs to happen in one day. Basically, we are doing this illegally," He told her.

"So, are you saying this is our only chance to have medical help and food sent through the wormhole? Is there a supply transport on its way?" She asked sounding alarmed.

"Lillian, the program has been shut down. They are not funding any other transports and they have no intentions of rescuing anyone in the colony. This is a covert rescue mission your mom has been fighting for and trying to get funded since she has been back," he explained.

"We'll be ready. Send the first pods through when you are able. I will be here and will get help."

The transmission ended and Commander Stanton began collecting all the medical supplies he had collected and brought to the station to pack into the pods. Ella stayed with Little David and organized the medical equipment and supplies into high level to low level needs. Then they sent the first few pods through.

35

THE RETURN

The last pod arrived. Ella waited in anticipation, wondering what her children and the man who had been her husband on the planet would think of her. Lillian Rose stepped from the first pod and she gazed at her daughter, trying to recognize the child's features in the young woman's face.

Her hair was braided down her back, in the style that Ella had always worn her hair while on a mission. Her hair had darkened to a brown color with hints of red, more like her father's darker hair instead of her own red hair. She gazed back at her mother with bright blue eyes, eyes that Ella adored looking into since they were the color of the sky she had missed for the years she was away from Earth. Then she smiled and she saw the reflection of her young child in the woman's face.

Lillian reached out her hand to the man in the pod. The hand that reached for her was the hand of an older man. He stood up and stepped from the pod. Lillian Rose took at deep breath as she gazed at her father, whose aged appearance remained but his struggles with arthritis had disappeared. Ella was mesmerized by the beautiful older man standing before her. Her heart skipped a beat and a tear slipped down her cheek upon seeing him.

As he looked at her all the emotions and distress he felt melted away. He walked towards Ella and placed his hands on her cheeks to look at her, gazing into he eyes of the woman who had been missing for twenty years. He leaned down his head and kissed her warmly, feeling the softness of her lips upon his own. Ella leaned into David, reveling in the feeling of his hands on her cheeks and having his lips merging with hers once again.

As she pulled away to look at him, she admired the silver hairs at his temples and brushed her fingers through them. He looked distinguished and mature. He was more attractive than she had remembered, seeing that his additional age added to his appearance. He saw the tears streaming down her face and smiled fondly at her.

"How much time passed here, my love?" David asked.

"Only a little over a year," she answered.

"And Martin?" He asked seriously. She sighed and looked down to the side away from him.

"It's complicated?" She stated hoping he would understand.

"It's always complicated," he said tersely.

"I had another child. He is yours," she announced to him. She turned to go into the adjoining room and picked up a small baby with red hair and fair skin, skin like his own.

"I love babies," he said as he lifted the babe from her arms. He snuggled the child and as the infant cooed in his sleep, David's heart melted.

"David, I was told I could never come back to you.

The mission was shut down. I have now broken all the regulations and am trespassing," she told him.

In that moment as he stood there gazing down at her with babe in arms, red and blue flashing lights illuminated her head like a halo.

36

BAIL OUT

Martin was with Ava when he got the call from the police station. He had to leave immediately to get the bail money to get her out of the county jail. Ava was miffed that another incident with Ella was happening, another situation that conveniently took Martin away from her. He kissed her quickly goodbye and rushed out the door.

When he got to the police station, he was not prepared to see a group of redheaded people that looked similar to Ella and an older man standing with a baby that looked strikingly like his son, David. Then the man turned his head and Martin saw that the older man was David, Ava's ex. Martin shriveled at the sight of the man. It didn't help that there were all these beautiful red haired people that looked like Ella standing around cooing over the baby.

He approached the counter to ask about Ella, ignoring the crew of people surrounding David. He quietly paid the money and stated he didn't need to see her. Then he slunk out of the police station being sure to hang back and watch as Ella was released.

She emerged and the women hugged her warmly, calling her mom. She took the baby in her arms and kissed David, leaning into him naturally, as if she belonged in his arms. In that moment, Martin saw that his son was not his own. Tears welled up in his eyes and he turned to leave and return home.

In their home, Martin wrote a brief note and left it on the kitchen counter. Then he called Ella and left a message stating he would not be home that evening and was going out of town on a business trip. He packed his clothes, as if he were going on a trip, and left for Ava's apartment.

Ava opened the door, not expecting to see Martin standing there distraught. He told her what he saw and his suspicions about the child. She embraced him and told him he could stay with her as long as he needed. She felt victorious.

Ella received the message on her phone and sighed in relief. She invited her family and David to come home with her until arrangements could be made for them. She arrived at the house ahead of her crew, her family, and put baby David in his high chair for the dinner she needed to prepare for him and serve him. On the counter she saw a letter with her name on the envelope scrawled in Martin's hand. She picked it up, shaking as she stared at it. Then she gingerly opened it.

Dear Ella,

I know things have been difficult between us for the past few months. I have not been what you needed. After seeing you in the police station, greeted by David as you walked out, it is clear that you must move on from our life together. So, I am going to make this easier for you, though it will hurt deeply.

I have been having an affair with Ava. I have not just been visiting my child. We have fallen I love and I hid that from you. She meets my needs in ways that you have not been able to. You have tried, but it is not in your nature to be the woman I need to have in my bed. Ava can fill that role. She has filled that role for me, completely.

When I am with her, I feel like I can be who I am meant to be. She allows me to be myself. When I am with you, I shrivel inside and have to force myself to be intimate with you. That is not to say I am not attracted to you, because I am. It is just that I do not feel the love I once felt for you.

I believe it would be best if I did not come home. I know little David is not my child. I will not fight you on that. You can keep the house, since it stands for the dream I had of having a family with you… a family you clearly have with David.

I wish you the best. I will send you the divorce papers stating I am at fault and that I had an affair.

Martin

37

HAPPILY EVER....?

The letter drifted to the floor as David walked up and put his arm around Ella. He could tell by the way her shoulders hunched over and her hands were trembling that something was wrong. He leaned into her and a tear dropped to his arm, permeating his sleeve.

"Shh. I've got you," David whispered to her. She leaned one hand on the counter and grabbed his arm with her other arm. She quietly wailed with a rattle that vibrated through her soul. He squeezed her firmly letting her know he was there

Their daughters and son were rattling in the background with each other, cooing to little David as he squealed in delight over all the attention from his siblings. Ella breathed in deeply, calming herself with the noise of her children chattering, calming herself with the firm embrace of David's arms around her. With a final rattling breathe she reached up and wiped the tears from her face with the sleeve of her sweater. Then she turned around and kissed David, the first real kiss upon his return.

When she pulled away their children were looking at them with glints in their eyes. The collection of red haired children gazing back at Ella looked like a family photo at Christmas, and she chuckled at the sight of them all together. In a moment, she had gone from a destructive marriage and a baby to a full family of children who loved and adored her with a man she knew cared for her completely.

MARTIN SPED off in his sports car, hugging the turns at top speed. The rain poured down, empathic to his emotions. He felt conflicted as he sped to Ava's apartment. As he drove he dialed Ava's cell to let her know that he had left Ella and was coming home to her.

"Hello?" Ava answered as she woke from a deep sleep. It wasn't her night with Martin and she had decided that a night on her own in a club would help her manage her jealousy over his marriage to Ella.

"I'm coming over! Ella is cheating on me!" Martin cried.

"Ella? But I thought she was doing research?" Ava mumbled then looked over as she heard the soft snoring of the man she'd brought home as her evening's playmate laying in the bed beside her.

"I need you tonight. I need to feel you wrapped around me," he stated.

"Martin, this isn't your night," Ava stated. She knew she would never have the time to get her play thing out of her bed and out of her house in time for when Martin would arrive to her door.

"I pay for your apartment. I am almost there and I need you tonight!" He said firmly.

"Martin, do not come over! You pay for this place to provide for your child, not to control me!" She insisted.

"I will fuck you when I want to fuck you!" He said as she heard the screeching of his wheels in her driveway. She hung up her phone, rushed to her bathroom and quickly wiped her mound with a wet rag, then rushed down to her living room. She positioned herself naked with her legs splayed leaning against the couch. She made herself look ready to take him into her the moment he entered into her door.

Martin threw open the door, saw her, and unzipped his pants pulling his member out quickly to ready himself for her.

"Get on your knees, woman," he ordered. "You disobeyed me and argued with me. You need to be punished."

"Yes, sir," she answered, praying that her playmate upstairs would not wake up and come out to find her.

Martin grabbed a handful of her hair and pulled her head back. Then he began to spank her, saying, "You have been so bad. Say you've been bad."

"I've been so bad," she told him as he spanked her harder, leaving a red mark on her rear.

"Say you want me to punish you," he ordered her as he grabbed her mound and pushed his fingers inside of her, rubbing her roughly.

"Please punish me for how bad I have been," she stated flatly, while trying to emote desire and passion in her voice. She glanced up toward the stairs and her bedroom door, hoping that it wouldn't open.

"Tell me you want me to punish you with a hard fuck," he ordered her, roughly massaging her and pulling her hair back tighter. She winced and let out a painful moan.

"Fuck me, sir. Punish me, sir," she said sounding like he

was already causing her pain. He got very hard by her sounds of pain and plunged himself into her immediately. He pounded into her, pulling her hips to him, digging his fingers into her hips.

"Tell me you want it harder," he stated pushing himself into her, as she winced in pain with every thrust.

"Harder, sir. Punish me harder," she said, biting her lip so she wouldn't yell out and wake up her visitor upstairs. He was beginning to hurt her, treat her in a way that she'd not experienced from him in a long time.

"You want more?"

"Yes, sir. I want more."

"You need more punishment," he said flatly as he pulled out of her. She was confused. Then she felt his fingers dig into her, slickly rub up her, and plunged into her ass. He stretched her, massaged her, and lubricated her briskly. Then he invaded her with a fast insertion into her ass. He pushed himself into her, stretching her, and thrusting quickly into her ass, screaming out in anger. He pulled out and went to clean himself off.

Ava lay there stunned, warm tears sliding down her face. In that moment, she realized he was punishing her for something Ella had done. She wondered when he would stop doing this, when he would stop punishing her for the issues he had in his marriage. Then she saw her house guest, her playmate, emerge from her bedroom.

"Miss Ava, what's going on? Are you okay?" He asked.

Martin came out from the restroom and looked up at the man at the top of the stairs. "Who the fuck is this?" He asked Ava.

"It wasn't your night, Martin," she answered flatly.

"You have a man in the apartment I pay for?" He asked.

"It wasn't your night."

He backhanded her, causing her lip to bleed. He'd never hit her before. "Every night is my night. Get him out of here. I don't want to see anyone else here when I get back." He stated as he zipped up his pants and left the apartment.

The rain poured down the windshield of his car as his engined revved in the dark night. He sped away, peeling down the street away from her apartment. He headed toward the curving heels, ready to bury his anger in the curves of the road under the tires of his fast car.

He approached the curve, racing at 90 miles per hour, turning his wheel to match the speed of his car. In a moment, he miscalculated the sharp turn, his back wheel catching the side of the asphalt, pulling him into the dirt at the side of the road. His tires lost traction and he slid off the road soaring over the edge of the cliff, briefly hanging in midair before gravity took over. The last thing Martin saw was the water sliding down his windshield whipping away to the edges and the moon glowing in the distance over the calm ocean.

THE PHONE RANG EARLY in the morning, which was unusual to Ella. When she answered it the police were on the other end. They told her they found her husband's car and the bottom of a cliff, that he had run off the road the night before, that his remains indicated he had died instantly. She stood there stunned, unable to say anything.

38

BURIAL AND WILL

Ella sat stunned at Martin's wake. His coworkers approached her one after the other to express how sorry they were for her loss. She just nodded her head trying to get through the night. David made the decision to stay at the house with their children and the baby. Handshake after handshake and questions of how people could help her wore on her nerves. She was about to retire to her seat when a woman reached for her hand.

"I am so sorry for your loss," Anna stated as she grabbed Ella's hand and placed her other hand on top of them. Ella looked up and gazed at Anna directly, feeling conflicted emotions of rage and relief at the same time. She sighed deeply to compose her thoughts.

"Thank you. I am sure it was also a loss for you," Ella said.

"Yes," Anna stated softly as tears welled into her eyes.

39

PROJECTION

The chime sounded softly from the clock as Alex gazed out to the gardens below. The light rain from the morning left raindrops on the delicate limbs that reflected the sunlight. She looked at the spiderweb with the tiny drops suspended in the air. Her mom used to love taking photos of spiderwebs with the morning dew hanging from the webs as she walked through trails in the forest.

Alex wished she'd had the chance to walk those trails with her mom. Her mom left journals of her morning hikes with sketches and photographs of plants and webs she came across. She felt like she knew her mom through those journals, the documentation of a botanist and lover of nature.

A tear slid down her face as she wished she had been given the chance to know her mysterious mom, who left journals of plants and webs, but no personal documentation of her life outside of her career. Alex knew her mom loved her father, from small tokens she found hidden in books and drawers after her passing. But there were no images, no words that acknowledged his existence or what happened between them. All she had of him was a newspaper article that covered the crash that killed him.

Alex hated that she felt sad on this day — a day she should be filled with happiness for her friend. But she instead reflected on the absence of a mother she barely knew. She remembered her small hand in her mom's hand as she took her to playdates. She remembered the day she felt a hot tear fall on her tiny hand, and looking up at her mom gazing at the horizon as the sun set with tears streaking down her face. It was the tears she remembered as the details of her mom's features vanished as she grew older. But she never forgot the tears reflecting the setting sun.

She heard the door open softly and quickly wiped away her tears. She expected to see her best friend, Lydia, enter with her wedding dress in a bustle of nerves. When she turned around she saw David closing the door and turning the lock.

"What are you doing?!" She whispered with distress.

"I needed to see you again," he answered plainly.

"You shouldn't be here." He crossed the room and kissed her passionately. She kissed him back as her desire rose for him.

He pushed the silky robe off her shoulders, revealing her ample breasts aching for attention. He looked down at her body, attired only in the delicate lace thong that accentuated the curve of her hips. He pressed her against the wall and empaled her with his shaft. The secrecy of the tryst excited her and she shuddered around him as he spilled into her.

He sighed and kissed her shoulder gently. She knew it was goodbye. He left her room as quietly as he came.

She looked over at the lavender dress hanging on the

hook. Then she sighed and sat down to write a quick note, handwritten. She placed it on the dress as she zipped her bag up and grabbed her plane ticket. She refused to be present when the chaos fell as quickly as the rain. But she knew the sun would burn it away like the dew on the spider's web, and she was going to be the mom she'd never had to the tiny babe she carried silently.

Made in the USA
Columbia, SC
27 September 2024